LEVELS OF EXPOSURE

The Distortion Series, Book 2

By Aimee McNeil

LEVELS OF EXPOSURE

Limitless Publishing, LLC
Kailua, HI 96734
www.limitlesspublishing.com

Formatting: Limitless Publishing

ISBN-13: 978-1-68058-923-8
ISBN-10: 1-68058-923-7

DEDICATION

This one is for my haters.

I hope you find lots of things to complain about and it makes you deliriously happy when you tear this up.

CHAPTER ONE

Stephanie

The sound of a woman crying roused Stephanie's attention. She felt like she was underwater as she tried to distinguish where the sound was coming from. When she tried to speak, her body wouldn't cooperate…her mouth felt numb and filled with cotton. If she could actually force words through her throat she figured they would be covered in blood as the sharp pains scraped at her raw flesh. Stephanie wanted to call out to the woman whose tears reflected her own turmoil. The woman's cries pulled at her heart and roused her mind, making it reel at a pace too fast for her uncooperative body.

A shadow crossed over her and Stephanie forced her eyes to open. The dim lamp light lit the room as she tried to focus her eyes. It was a struggle to keep her lids open as her dry eyes worked against her, continually closing, making her find the strength to force them open again. Movement in her small cell caused adrenaline to aid her struggle. Stephanie blinked her eyes in confusion when she saw the blurry image of a woman in the corner, huddled in the shadow.

Stephanie forced words up her torn throat. "Wh…nooo…" Her tongue felt too large for her mouth and refused to let her words pass. Stephanie closed her eyes tight against the pain before trying to speak again. When she opened them, the corner of the cell was empty and she was alone. Her eyes frantically searched the entire cell. A deep chill flashed across her skin, permeating her to the bone until her insides began to shake. Tears filled her eyes but she couldn't lift her hands to wipe them away as they ran down her cheeks. The drugs made it hard to determine what was real and what was not.

Stephanie had no idea how much time had passed. She was constantly in a drug-induced state. She knew her captor was drugging her food…it didn't take her long to discover that she would lose consciousness shortly after she ate the food he left outside her cell. At first she didn't mind it. She preferred to sleep instead of stare through the bars at the man who watched her silently from across the room. He wouldn't give her answers. He would only stare at her with his dark mind churning behind those eyes that were anything but human. He seemed to be waiting for her tears. It was only then that his unmoving form would start to rouse, slowly rubbing his hands up and down his thighs. The more she cried, the more he enjoyed watching her. She gave up demanding him to tell her why she was here and pleading to let her go. All of her promises to never tell fell on deaf ears. This man did not intend to let her go.

His routine was beginning to change and Stephanie feared what this meant for her. She remembered a bright light shining in her face; it was too bright to open her eyes. She tried to turn away but realized her arms were bound to her sides. Stephanie closed her eyes, trying to stop the memory from assaulting her. She wanted to drift back into nothingness, with so many drugs still in her system, it was easy to submit to sleep.

The sensation of warm water trickling on her skin caused her to flinch, and she stretched her legs, pulling at firm straps that bound her feet. She was completely immobile and the fear jolted her awake. She lifted her head to see those dark eyes watching her. She couldn't stop the tears that exploded with devastation. She was strapped to some kind of metal table, completely naked. Screams followed her tears as she fought with the ties binding her.

His eyes flared as he squeezed the sponge in his hand, and water poured onto her. He began to rub the sponge in gentle circles against her leg while she struggled and tried to fight him unsuccessfully. "No...don't do this, please...please!" Stephanie begged.

She cried as he slowly washed her, using small gentle strokes as he meticulously covered every inch of her skin. Then he smoothed shaving cream on her legs before pulling a razor up the length of her shin. Stephanie jerked her leg and the sting of the blade burned across her skin.

"Look what you did, Rose," he said, shaking his head. "You shouldn't have done that." It was the first time he had spoken to her in what seemed like forever. His voice was strangely normal. She had imagined if he ever did say anything to her again it would sound evil, inhuman, because she couldn't imagine a person capable of this. Instead, it was the first time she considered that this man might have the world fooled. Fear that no one would suspect him of evil made her shudder. What if no one ever came looking for her? The realization struck her that these dark confines might be the last place she ever knew. She could feel her last traces of hope slip through her fingers.

"My name isn't Rose," Stephanie gasped through her tears.

"Don't be foolish," he said as he grabbed a cloth and pressed it to her knee to stop the blood. "You don't want to make me angry, do you, Rose?"

A soft whimper escaped her throat as she shook her head no.

"Good girl. You're just confused after what had happened."

She retreated inside her head as he continued to shave her legs. She refused to give him any reaction as he worked on her, preparing her for something she could not let herself think about. Stephanie closed her eyes as warm water poured over her hair and then winced as his fingers began massaging soap into her scalp. The fruity scent filled her nose as she tried to block out her senses.

She thought about Lexie and Evan and

desperately hoped they were well. Thoughts of Lexie in this same situation threatened to break her. She focused on their faces, keeping them close as she searched for strength. She thought of her parents and their last conversation when they asked her to come for dinner that weekend. Her mother was making her favorite pasta dish and she tried to remember the excitement she felt when she was looking forward to eating until she was ready to explode, like every time she was treated to her mother's cooking. She didn't know if the weekend had already come and gone. She wondered if her parents knew she was missing and if they were looking for her. Her mother always worried about her, always fussing over the smallest details when it came to her only daughter.

She thought of her boyfriend, Mike. They had barely spoken the last week before she had been taken. He hadn't come home in three days because he had been staying with his friend. The last time they were together they had argued about the fact he had been hanging out at the local strip bar. She realized he had been lying to her when she heard a rumor that he had been seen throwing up outside The Lighthouse. The strip bar consisted of nothing more than a rundown building and pathetic display of talent upon the stage. She was more embarrassed than angry when she confronted him. Their last words to each other were harsh and she wondered if that would be how he remembered her.

Stephanie had no idea how much time had passed, not knowing when one day turned into the next. She had so many things she wanted the people in her life to know and the realization that she would never see them again made her squeeze her eyes shut against the assaulting waves of pain.

Stephanie stared at the dingy ceiling as he ran a comb through her hair, over and over. She tried to make her body numb and allow her mind to go somewhere else, but no matter how hard she tried, her fear kept her aware of what was happening. She was forced to endure every moment.

She was surprised to feel relief when she saw a syringe in his hand. The prick of pain as he pushed it through her skin was welcomed as she closed her eyes and felt herself drift away.

Stephanie looked down at her small cell, the cot in the corner, with the thin wrinkled sheet hanging off the edge, the dirtied floor and the bucket in the corner. She was looking down at herself sitting on the bed, arms wrapped around her knees. She tried to scream out to herself but she couldn't speak, she couldn't move. She could only watch herself cry in her misery.

She watched herself lift her head and lean back against the concrete wall and that was when Stephanie realized it was not herself she was looking at, her features were undeniably similar but she knew it wasn't her. She wondered how many others were locked in this cell. She could feel the despair as real as the bars caging her in. Stephanie wanted to ask who she was but she was unable to do anything but observe no matter how hard she fought. A force kept her just out of Stephanie's reach.

"Wake up." Stephanie felt a gentle touch on her shoulder, so soft she thought she imagined it. She could feel a small protest bubble from her chest. "Wake up! He's coming." This time she could feel someone grasp her shoulders and give a shake. Stephanie jolted from sleep, pushing herself up to a sitting position. She pushed her back against the wall, brought her knees up to her chest, and wrapped her arms tightly around them. She couldn't shake the disturbing dream. It had felt so real. The woman's voice still floated around in her thoughts as she searched for her. She could still feel her hands on her shoulders. She reached up and placed her hands over the lingering sensation and sought comfort in the fact for the first moment since she arrived she didn't feel so alone in this hell.

The sound of the lock sliding in the door made Stephanie's heart race, she could feel her pulse in her throat as she lay down and pretended to be asleep. She concentrated on slowing her breath to deep, even intervals, trying to block out the sound of his footsteps across the floor.

His wedding band clinked against the bars but he remained quiet, watching her. "I know you're awake, Rose," he said after a stretch of time. The drugs in her system were wreaking havoc on her thoughts. She wasn't sure how long had passed or if she had fallen asleep and this was another dream. She desperately wanted it to be a dream. She didn't want to look at his face anymore and wonder if today would be the day he decided to kill her.

Stephanie opened her eyes and looked at him. He was dressed in a suit with his tie loosened and

7

hanging haphazardly around his neck, his haunting eyes never leaving her. His clothes looked expensive and she couldn't' help but wonder who he was when he left here. She wondered what woman would be married to a man like him and if she feared him like Stephanie did.

"There you are." He smiled at her, an expression that seemed unnatural for his face. "You need to eat, Rose." He pointed to a tray of food she hadn't touched. The wonderful smells had called to her but she couldn't take any more drugs. She didn't know what was real or not anymore.

"No more drugs…they make me feel so sick," Stephanie whispered. She could feel the physical toll weighing heavily on her exhausted body.

"As long as you behave I don't need to drug you." He unlocked the cell door and then picked up the tray. Walking inside, he approached her bed and sat down, placing the tray on the edge. "Do you promise to behave?"

Stephanie nodded her head and tried not to tremble. She didn't want to show fear but it poured out of her regardless.

He placed a hand on her arm and then ran it over the length of her body. "Good girl," he said. "Good girl." Stephanie squeezed her eyes shut and held her breath until she felt the weight of his body leave the bed and the sound of the cell door closing behind him.

CHAPTER TWO

Jackson

"I'm not fucking staying here!"

"Calm down, Mr. Wethers."

"Don't tell me to calm the fuck down. *You* calm the fuck down."

Jackson and Teddy both glanced at each other as they walked down the hospital hallway toward Dane's room, where the voices originated from. A large grin spread across Teddy's face and Jackson shook his head in disbelief.

"What the fuck did you do, Teddy?"

"Mansfield was the only available officer."

"You are such a fucking child." Jackson sighed as he slowed in front of Dane's open door.

A nurse was standing in front of Dane, visibly trying to calm his fired temper. Mansfield stood against the wall, beads of sweat visibly breaking out across his forehead. He pushed his glasses up his nose nervously and shuffled his feet.

"Please sit down, Mr. Wethers. You're going to

9

injure yourself again." The frazzled nurse looked exhausted as she pleaded with Dane. Her grey hair was working free of her bun and frayed around her tired face.

Jackson cleared his throat to alert the room of their arrival and leaned against the doorframe, crossing his arms. Everyone in the room turned to address them.

"Please don't let us intrude. Carry on," Teddy said encouragingly.

Dane pointed his finger at Teddy with a glare, showcasing his rage. "You had something to do with this, didn't you? If I have to listen to one more second of this idiot's theories about video games and government he came up with living in his mother's basement, I'm gonna shoot myself in the head, and then I will fucking come after you too," Dane threatened Teddy.

"You do see the obvious flaw in your plan, right?" Teddy continued to instigate Dane's already ruffled feathers.

"Teddy, take Mansfield for a coffee or something."

"Oh come on," Teddy complained.

"We don't have time for this shit, Ted," Jackson warned. Teddy was well aware of the situation.

"Fine." Teddy waved for Officer Mansfield to follow him. "Come on, Manny."

Officer Mansfield pushed off the wall hesitantly, his eyes remaining on Dane as he moved toward the door. His hands visibly shook, along with his round belly hanging over his belt. Mansfield was still relatively young, but he was built like a man that spent most of his life sitting at a desk. His strength was his mind, leaving his body underutilized. "Do you want me to bring you back a coffee and magazine?" Mansfield's high voice wobbled slightly as he addressed Dane.

Dane's eyes flared before he growled out in frustration. Mansfield backed out of the room without another word. Teddy grabbed his shoulder and began leading him down the hallway. "So tell me, Manny, is your mom hot?"

Jackson closed his eyes and took a deep breath before turning back toward Dane. He had to give Office Mansfield some credit; although the man was as socially awkward as they came, he was a good officer. He knew the rule book like a priest knew the bible and lived within the lines. He saw the world through a set of lenses that were uniquely his, and for some reason he looked up to Dane, always trying to impress him despite the fact that Dane's patience for him was nonexistent.

"Get me out of here, Jackson." Dane's gaze was full of meaning. Jackson knew Dane could only stand so much alone time before he would go stir crazy and apparently the company of Officer Mansfield was no better. He obviously had reached his limit, looking like he was ready to crawl out of his skin.

"Slap a fresh bandage on him, we're taking him home," Jackson told the nurse.

"His doctor hasn't released him yet."

"I don't care. He's leaving," Jackson said abruptly.

"But…" the nurse began to argue but trailed off

11

when she sensed Jackson's impatience. "He'll have to sign a waiver. I'll go get the paperwork ready."

The nurse slipped out of the room. Jackson swung the door closed behind her.

"It took you long enough." Dane rubbed his hands down his face. His frayed edges were exposed from being confined to the small, bare room. Though he never admitted it, Jackson knew Dane had a fear of small spaces. He always chose the stairs instead of an elevator, no matter the amount of stairs he had to face, and he spent more time outside than anyone Jackson knew. Something about being confined by four walls and a ceiling never sat well with Dane. The three of them made quite the dysfunctional team, never wanting to talk about a past that haunted them and far too comfortable walking the line of danger to ever be mistaken for normal. They all worked together like a well-oiled machine, however, always getting results. It was the only reason Giles put up with them.

"We were following a lead on Stodden, you know that."

"Yeah...well, they sent a fucking head doctor down to see me. She wanted me to talk about my feelings and shit."

"And?"

"She was fucking hot. The only feeling I had was in my pants."

"Is there any other kind?"

"It's the only kind I care to think about," Dane said as he grabbed his phone and his personal effects off the bedside table. "Shit, I need clothes."

"Here." Jackson held out a bag. "Figured you wouldn't want to walk out of here with your dress on." Jackson nodded toward Dane's hospital gown.

"You're a funny guy, Ace," Dane said sarcastically as he grabbed the bag and pulled out a pair of jeans. "So tell me what happened at the warehouse."

"It was a bust. John had wiped his prints off the whole operation. Haffey and her team are back to square one. No sign of Stodden or the girls."

Dane turned and looked up at Jackson with narrowed eyes. "This doesn't seem to faze you. What's your plan?"

Jackson rubbed the back of his neck thoughtfully. "I'm not gonna get Stodden by playing by the rules," he admitted. "I'm gonna take a new approach."

"Teddy?" Dane asked as he pulled on his pants, carefully minding his side.

"He's with me."

"How are you keeping Giles in the dark?"

"I have no clue, but I think I can stretch a few days without raising flags. Teddy's little number said she would keep us on the paperwork a few extra days at the Belhaven Precinct."

"So his little side bone is proving to be useful." Dane laughed. "What's your plan?"

"I'm going to pay Max a visit," Jackson confessed, knowing Dane would have the same hesitance as Teddy did when it came to Max. Jackson hadn't spoken to Max since he had called him to clean up the bodies at Stephanie's house. Since he hadn't heard otherwise, he assumed it was taken care of. Max was a contact Jackson had come to know through living on the streets before he pursued a badge. He kept in touch over the years, knowing that a contact on the other side of the law would benefit him one day. He just didn't realize how soon that need would come.

Dane pulled his shirt over his head and gently down over his bandage. "You sure that's wise? That guy is as shady as they come."

"I already owe him. I'm just gonna make sure I get my money's worth," Jackson confessed.

"Hell...count me in. Beats lying around and doing nothing. Giles said I'm off for a few weeks, no exceptions."

"How's your trigger finger?"

Dane lifted his hand in the air and gave his index finger a wiggle. "She's sweet as candy."

"And your side?"

Dane looked down at his side. "After the little run in with Stodden's man, I'm a little tore up, but what's life without a little pain?" He gently placed his hand over the bandage. "Plus they are giving me killer meds."

Since their warning hadn't come soon enough for Dane, he had to face the man John Stodden sent to kill him alone. Although at the time he was recovering from his surgery, Dane fought off the man's attempt and ultimately killed him. Unfortunately, it landed him back in the operating room. Dane's attacker was Carlton Myers. He was a man who had been in and out of prison his entire life with no legitimate job and no family that claimed him. He fit the profile of Stodden's men perfectly, but not even he could be traced back to John Stodden without reasonable doubt. Stodden had a way of evading detection that proved he had many people in his bed. They just needed to find out who was in his fold and find a way to make them talk.

"You don't have to join us, you know. You could sit this one out."

The door opened and Teddy walked in with his usual carefree demeanor. "What's up?"

Dane ignored him and continued his conversation with Jackson. "Even half broke I'm still better than Teddy anyway. You need me."

"Fuck you," Teddy responded with a shake of his head. "All you do is point and shoot. Any idiot can fire a gun." Teddy couldn't keep the smile off his face.

"Calm down, children." Jackson smiled. He had been wound so tight lately it was nice to take the edge off. The last few days he'd barely slept. He had spent those last few days rounding out his time at Belhaven so he wouldn't rouse suspicions by ducking out of town too soon. During that time Jackson absorbed as much information as he could about what they had on Stodden, which was file after file of dead ends. On paper, Stodden looked like a business genius. His hand was in many different pots, all of which turned a considerable profit. Underneath this façade, Jackson knew, were the dark, inner workings. He only needed to find the weak spot and crack Stodden's whole operation wide open. Then he would take down Stodden and bring the girls home. Make sure Lexie was safe.

Thoughts of Lexie haunted him. Every time he closed his eyes, all he could see was her beautiful face with those fear-filled eyes. He was tormented by the fact that he didn't protect her. She had trusted him and he not only allowed her to be taken, but he revealed a truth that was unforgiveable. He knew the girl who would come home from this would not be the same girl who looked to him for answers or who saw something in him that he didn't know existed. Part of him was relieved that bridge was already burned. Now he wouldn't have to look her in the eye and tell her they could be nothing more than what they were. He knew he wouldn't have the strength to walk away from her given the choice.

"You in?" Teddy asked Dane.

"Someone has to watch Jackson's back. You get distracted too easily with flashing lights."

"It was one time *and* there were strippers involved. You can't blame me for that. Right, Jacks?" Teddy said defensively.

"No man," Jackson confirmed. "I'm still here, aren't I?"

"Because of me," Dane said confidently. "So goes my argument that you need me."

"Where's Mansfield?" Jackson asked, noting Teddy was alone.

"I told him that we could take it from here. He seemed a little hesitant to leave his boyfriend in our care, but what can I say? I can talk anyone into doing what I want." Teddy smiled proudly.

"Don't call him my boyfriend," Dane bit off.

"Hey now, you're not giving Mansfield enough

credit. Did you know he builds train sets? He has a whole basement filled with tiny models and shit. I think he even mentioned he has a little figure of you and him holding hands and skipping through the park."

"Let's get out of here." Dane rolled his eyes. "I need some strong coffee."

"Why do you have such strong hatred for our good buddy, Manny, anyway?" Teddy asked, all humor dying away from his voice.

Dane took a deep breath and looked at Teddy for a moment. Jackson could see his inner struggle. "No reason. I just can't stand idiots," Dane said, throwing Teddy a dirty look. He pushed past Teddy and pulled open the door. Dane was similar to his weapon of choice. He was a loaded gun and it was not wise to toy with his trigger.

"To the bat cave," Teddy said as they followed Dane into the hallway.

Not knowing where Lexie was or if she was well slowly picked away at Jackson's sanity. He needed a clear head to confront this beast. He knew that somewhere in getting to Mary Connors and bringing down John Stodden he would uncover the truth about his father's murder. There was not one sole person in this scenario that was to blame. He realized his father's death was the result of him looking into John Stodden all those years ago. His last case was the reason he no longer walked this earth and Stodden was the mastermind that stopped him.

Mary's confession that Rosh, his father's partner, was the person that actually pulled the trigger planted a seed of doubt in his mind. There had always been something that did not sit well about Rosh's retelling of the events of that night. A few inconsistencies that Jackson had filed away that now were beginning to make sense with this new piece of information, though the very thought of accusing Rosh was hard to swallow.

Rosh had always been like family. Always checking up on him and his mother after his father died. Making sure they had food when his mother couldn't bring herself to leave the house. He was the one that attended Jackson's ball games growing up. He had been there when his mother died, visiting him at Giles and always checking in to make sure he had what he needed. He didn't want to believe the man that seemed so disheartened by the loss of his partner, Jackson's father, could be the one who killed him.

Jackson knew things were not always what they seem. This life had a way of turning people against each other. Everyone had a breaking point. He just needed to find a reason why Rosh would have turned on his father. He knew if he followed this path it would also lead him to John Stodden's door, reaffirming his plan to tear that very man to the ground and burn his remains.

CHAPTER THREE

Lexie

It had been almost a week since Lexie was blindfolded and forced into the back of the vehicle and brought to this prison. The soft sheets, feather pillows, and expensive paintings on the wall did nothing to distract from the truth of the situation. She no longer saw any of it as she stared out the window facing the endless horizon of trees. There were no landmarks, or distinguishing elements to indicate their possible location. She had no way of knowing where John had taken her and her mother.

Her mind would not let her rest, especially where Jackson was concerned. John's words swirled in her mind about what Jackson's true intentions were, but they were at war with what her heart wanted to believe. She hoped she would have the opportunity to confront Jackson. All the words she wanted to say to him formed a hard knot in her stomach and left her confused. She didn't know why she let Jackson so close that he could affect her like this.

19

Every day that passed she was no closer to finding a solution, and it carved away at her hope. Her leash was so short, it was nonexistent. John had refused to let her leave the room since the first day.

The only time she was allowed to see her mother was that first night when she attended dinner with John. The memory of it sat heavy in her chest.

"Who are you?" Lexie questioned the man that walked into her room. His dark eyes dropped from her face and slid down the length of her dress without the courtesy of discretion. Lexie clenched her fists at her side despite the desire to cross her arms over herself and hide from his prying eyes. "Who are you?"

"You can call me Flint. I'm here to escort you to dinner." He looked to be a few years younger than John, ten at the most, but not as well manicured despite wearing a suit. There was a rawness to him that made him seem more like a wild animal that learned to play nice when the situation called for it. He had salt and pepper hair with an unshaven face and a look in his eye that gave Lexie a heavy dose of fear.

Lexie cleared her throat. "Right...okay. I'm ready," she confirmed.

Flint came closer and Lexie forced her feet to remain planted despite her instinct to flee, her head filled with warning bells. His eyes never left hers and she was scared to be the first to look away and show any weakness.

When he held out his arm Lexie hesitated, not wanting any physical contact with this man. He was like a snake waiting to strike but she needed to appear cooperative for the time being. She couldn't afford any more obstacles in her way. She tentatively placed her hand on his arm but Flint pulled her closer, a sly smile curling his lips.

"I won't bite...yet." He grinned wickedly. Lexie instinctively tried to pull away but Flint refused to loosen his hold on her. "What's the matter? Do I make you nervous?"

"No, I was just thinking how unoriginal your joke was. I won't bite yet? You'd think someone your age would come up with something better than that," Lexie challenged.

"Ouch." Flint feigned hurt. "You're feistier than I realized. I like it."

"Well, just to be clear, I don't like you," Lexie said defiantly. "Shouldn't we leave? I don't want to keep John waiting." Lexie couldn't care less if John waited a thousand years, but she knew her mother was also joining them and she needed to know she was well, not to mention she couldn't stand the man in her current company. Like John, Flint gave her the feeling that something horrible was about to happen.

"Very well." Flint led her out of the room and down the hall. Lexie tried to take note of her surroundings, trying to find clues to where they were, except everything was stripped bare and recently painted. The distinct chemical smell filled her senses. They passed numerous doors lining the hallway, identical except for the numbers. Large sheets of plastic closed off some areas that looked to be under construction.

They approached a set of elevators. Two men Lexie recognized from the diner acknowledged Flint as he approached. The bald one, intimidating by his sheer size, pressed the down button when he noticed their arrival. Lexie didn't utter a word. Instead, she took the opportunity to study the men that held her captive, looking for a sign that one of them may be possibly sympathetic to a kidnapped girl and her mother. Unfortunately, she might as well have been invisible to these men.

They followed Lexie and Flint onto the elevator and didn't even give her a second glance when they stepped inside and turned their backs to her. The elevator only descended one floor before the doors opened and they filed out into an identical area as the floor above. Flint still refused to let Lexie retract her arm, holding her close against his side while gently stroking her hand. She tried not to think about his touch and the disturbing feelings it roused in her stomach.

They approached a set of double doors that opened into what looked like a banquet hall. Three large ornate chandeliers ran the length of the ceiling with large exposed beams. The wall color was a rich buttercream with large wall insets that framed beautiful paintings. The room looked fit for royalty with its fine details.

Lexie looked at the lone table situated in the center of the room. The bright white table cloth stood out in stark contrast. A beautiful bouquet of white roses sat in the center of the table surrounded by candles. Their footsteps echoed in the large space as they approached the table. Lexie noticed only two place settings. "John said my mother was joining us. Where is she?" Lexie looked around the room.

"She'll be here soon, I assure you." Flint took her hand in his and brought it up to his lips. Lexie tried not to pull away as he placed a kiss upon her hand. His warm lips felt disturbing and she just wanted the unpleasant exchange to be over. She was relieved when he finally released her.

Flint pulled out a chair for Lexie. "Thank you," she said tightly as she took the seat. Lexie nervously played with the edge of the tablecloth as she waited in the deafening silence, while Flint and the others kept watch over her. She was about to crawl out of her skin as she fidgeted under their gazes. "Where's John?" Lexie's words barely left her lips before John entered the room. He wore a different suit than he had been wearing earlier, this one looked more stylishly cut and appropriate for evening attire. She suddenly wished she had worn her dirty clothes to see what kind of reaction she would have gotten. He seemed to take personal appearances seriously. Her gaze stayed on the doorway behind John as he approached, hoping her mother would follow soon.

Lexie stood up abruptly when he neared, shoving her chair and causing it to scrape loudly along the floor. "You said my mother would be joining us. Where is she?" Lexie demanded.

John ignored her outburst. "You can wait outside," John dismissed Flint and the others.

Flint nodded, signaling the other two men to follow as they headed toward the door.

John pulled out his chair, his cold dark gaze landed on her. "Sit, Lexie."

Lexie stared back defiantly at him for a moment. It went against her nature to obey this man but she knew it would not be wise to aggravate a bear without having an escape plan in place. She was at a huge disadvantage and she needed to keep her head for the time being. Lexie pulled her chair in and sat down. John waited until she was settled before he unbuttoned his suit jacket and hung it over the back of his chair and took his seat. She decided it was best to wait for him to start the conversation since she already seemed to have crossed a line. She wasn't sure if he was willing to entertain any of her questions as he looked at her thoughtfully.

Lexie turned when she heard the sound of a door opening across the room. A waiter entered, pushing a metal cart. He stood obediently by the door until John waved him to approach. The man, dressed in a suit and bow tie, pushed the cart toward their table. He filled their water glasses and offered a choice of red or white wine. Lexie declined both wine choices and opted for water only. John, on the other hand, requested the red wine.

John took a generous sip and leaned back in his chair. "Your mother is being difficult."

"Well, you did kidnap her at gunpoint," Lexie said sarcastically. "I think difficult would be expected."

Lexie was surprised to hear John laugh. It was a gesture of which she didn't think him capable. She could feel the scowl form upon her brow as she leaned forward in her chair and grabbed hold of the edge of the table. "Where is she?"

"She's close," he confirmed. "How are you finding your room?"

"You mean my cell?" Lexie questioned with raised brows. "You tell me. I noticed your peeping tom camera."

"Those cameras are inactive. They were installed long before it was your room. As for having to be confined to your room…"John tilted his head with a frown. "I can't have you running off now, can I?"

"I'd be okay with it," Lexie said flatly. "In fact, I'd be okay with you letting us go."

"I can't do that, Lexie." John reached across the table to touch her hand but Lexie pulled it away before he could make contact. "What has your mother told you about me?"

"Nothing. She never told me about you and now I can see why." Lexie watched him clench his jaw. She was testing his patience but she couldn't help herself. He had to expect that she wasn't just going to accept being taken against her will.

"I understand your hesitance toward me, Lexie. In time you will learn how things work around here. Fighting me will do you no good," John's said casually.

"I don't like being kept in the dark. I want answers and you want my cooperation. I'm sure we can work something out." Lexie squared her shoulders, trying to make her small stature seem more imposing.

John rubbed his chin thoughtfully before pursing

his lips. *"What do you want to know?"*

"I want to know that Evan and Stephanie are home and safe from all of this."

John raised his hands in surrender. *"I don't have your friends, Lexie. As for their whereabouts, I cannot say. I pulled my men out of the area once we left the diner. They were no longer my concern. I already told you this."*

"I have trust issues," Lexie said as she tried to hide her relief. She wanted to believe him, she didn't know if it was because she was so desperate for it to be true or the look in his eye that conveyed his sincerity. *"What did my mother take from you that you want so badly?"* Lexie pressed on for more information while she had the chance.

John leaned forward and folded his hands on the top of the table. *"Your mother took a substantial amount of cash,"* John said casually. *"She betrayed me."*

Lexie narrowed her eyes. *"I highly doubt you would go to this much trouble over cash. You're obviously not hurting in that area, based on what I've seen. What did she take that you would hunt my mother down twenty-three years later?"*

"It's the principle."

Lexie shook her head. *"There's something you're not telling me,"* Lexie said as she tapped her fingers on the table.

The waiter presented Lexie with the first plate, removing the metal cover to reveal a beautifully arranged plate of steak and vegetables. Lexie's mouth watered from the delicious aroma. Hunger hit her hard and fast now that her body was *reminded it needed food.*

A sly smile spread across John's face. "Eat your dinner, Lexie."

"Let me talk to her. I'll ask her about what she took," Lexie said hopefully.

"Eat." John banged his fist upon the table, startling her. The dishes on the table rattled with the impact and Lexie was surprised their glasses were still upright. Even the waiter jumped back a few feet from the outburst. He grabbed hold of his cart and left quickly.

John's scowl quickly melted from his face as he picked up his knife and began carving into the steak upon his plate. "Chef Fortworth makes the most delectable steak. It is so tender that the knife just slides through it beautifully." He placed a piece in his mouth and chewed slowly before he swallowed.

Once the shock of his outburst wore off, Lexie picked up her utensils and began eating mechanically, unable to enjoy the flavours of the food as she remained under John's piercing gaze. His mood changed dramatically and the air around her felt chilled and unnatural. Lexie picked at her food, unable to stomach much despite the fact that she was hungry.

When John finished, he picked up his napkin, wiped his face, and then sipped his wine.

"Flint!" he hollered abruptly, causing Lexie's fork to slip from her hand and tumble to the floor with a loud clatter. She turned to see Flint enter the room a moment later. "Bring in Mary." John never took his eyes off Lexie.

Lexie watched the doorway expectantly, sitting

on the edge of her seat. She gasped when Flint led her mother into the room. Even at a distance she could see the blood staining the front of her mother's shirt. "Mom!" Lexie called. She moved to stand but John grabbed her hand across the table and held her firm.

"Lexie!" her mother called back, struggling against Flint's hold. Flint pulled out his gun and held it her mother's temple, ceasing her struggle. She gasped in terror as she stared at Lexie across the room.

John's hold on Lexie's hand was painful as she watched her mother being held at gunpoint. Lexie covered her mouth with her other hand, trying not to make a sound. John was showing her that he held all the power. She had no choice but to fold—for now.

"I will decide when you talk to your mother," John's words dripped with malice. When he released her hand, lingering pain radiated up the length of her arm. "I decide what becomes of you, remember this." John stood up and grabbed his jacket off the back of the chair. "That will be all, Flint."

Lexie stared after her mother as Flint led her out of sight, but her mother's haunted expression never left her.

"The moment I discovered you existed was the moment you lost your freedom," John said heartlessly. "You will learn to accept this." The two men that had ridden the elevator with her and Flint appeared and approached their table. Neither of them could pass as anything but criminals, with *their tattoos and harsh features. Everything about them built a case that they were less than upstanding citizens, unlike John, whose evil lurked under the surface—dark and vicious. "Take Lexie back to her room," John said, his eyes never leaving hers. Lexie never thought she would be relieved to go back to that room, but she was.*

Lexie had been confined to her room since John's men brought her back here, staring at the gift that had been left on her bed. It had been waiting for her when she returned. A beautiful red bow was tied perfectly around the decorative box but she refused to touch it, scared of what it might contain. The only time she saw someone was when food was delivered or when Flint stopped in and checked on her. She never paid attention to the time, drifting in and out of sleep, on edge waiting for something to happen. She wasn't sure what to expect or if this was her new life, existing in this box, waiting for everything and nothing at the same time.

All she had was the fear that boiled away in her stomach minute after minute with no idea what was happening to her mother. She wanted to claw through the walls and break free of this place. Emotions swelled so deep it was hard to keep them contained without feeling her sanity slipping.

Lexie stared at the perfectly wrapped gift box still sitting on her bed. She hadn't touched it. She hadn't slept on the bed. Instead, she curled up on the oversized chair in the corner of the room, as far away from the door as she could manage. She couldn't let her mind relax enough to fall into a proper sleep. Her nights were filled with restless dreams and she would jolt from sleep with the slightest sound, terrified someone would enter her room without her knowledge. She couldn't let her guard down. There were too many dangers lurking in John's world.

Lexie collapsed in the chair. She could no longer see anything else in the room except for the blood red bow, sitting there mocking her.

She walked over to the bed and sat on the edge. She grabbed the ribbon and pulled it closer. She pulled the cover off before she lost her nerve and looked inside. Lexie was surprised to see a beautiful camera. It was the exact model she had been saving for. She ran her fingers over the letters spelling Olympus on the top of the camera. A jar sat on the middle of her table in her apartment with a picture of this very camera. She had fallen in love with it since she had seen it in the display case at her favorite camera shop.

Now it was tainted, John had taken that dream from her like he did everything else. Lexie pulled it out of the box and felt it in her hands. She missed the rush of taking pictures but she refused to immortalize any moment of this hell she was currently living. Anger burned hot in her stomach, threatening to melt her. Lexie reeled her hand back and threw the camera into the television as hard as she could. The screen of the television exploded upon impact with a deafening crack.

CHAPTER FOUR

Jackson

Jackson pulled into the narrow driveway of an old, decrepit brick building. It was located in the part of the city he would otherwise avoid. Necessity was the only reason he stepped back into the part of Belhaven that housed his dark past...a childhood he couldn't seem to shake. It followed him like a living shadow. Jackson could already feel the change in the air; it tasted different and coated his throat, making it feel tight.

He pulled the car around back where the driveway opened up into a small parking lot hidden from street view. A couple of boys were playing basketball on the far side of the lot. Their net was a plastic garbage can with the bottom removed that they had secured on the metal bars of the fire escape.

Jackson turned off his car and looked out the window at the wary faces observing their arrival. An older gentleman stood on a small balcony a few floors up with a cigar hanging from his mouth. They man's oversized stomach was exposed and pressed against the railing, molding around the bars. He cast them an accusatory glare. He had seen far too many illegal transgressions happening in his building to be anything but suspicious of new faces.

"Something tells me we're not going to get a warm welcome here," Teddy said, looking at the few grim faces that were now looking out their windows, or closing their curtains.

"What are you talking about? This place reminds me of home sweet home," Dane said in a flat tone. "At least here you know what you're walking into."

"Let's get this over with," Jackson said, opening his door. He walked around the back of his car and opened the trunk to retrieve a backpack. He swung it over his shoulder and slammed it shut. Teddy was quick to follow, while Dane took his time climbing out of the back of the car, trying not to agitate his injury.

"Come on, old man," Teddy pestered. "The vultures will start circling if you don't move faster."

"Fuck you," Dane said, joining them at the door. "Let me shoot you in the stomach and see how fast you move."

The interior of the building smelled sour and musky as they walked toward the elevator. The walls were stained and damaged in areas. Property upkeep was not a priority for the owner of this building, it was deteriorating like the people that lived within. A few gaunt looking females were lingering in the lobby, desperation cast upon their features. A little flare of life sparked in their dull eyes but was quick to fade when they were ignored. "Ah...shit, Jackson. What floor are we going to?" Dane asked as they neared the elevators.

"The very top, man," Jackson said apologetically.

"Guess you'll have to ride the death trap with us 'cause your sorry ass won't make it up all those stairs." Teddy laughed at Dane's obvious discomfort with the situation.

"No fucking way I'm getting in that box. This building is as old as shit. It will probably get stuck. I'll stay right here," Dane insisted. He leaned against the wall with his arms crossed.

Jackson and Teddy stepped into the elevator. "We won't be long," Jackson assured him as the metal doors closed.

The top floor was in the same condition as the first, the entire interior needed to be gutted and sanitized. From the smells permeating into the halls, this place would be a good location for a drug raid. They passed a man slumped against the wall, snoring loudly. His shirt was torn and stained and he held a can of beer that had tipped over and saturated the carpeted floor. They stepped over him as they continued warily down the hall.

A small child, no more than three years old, was wandering toward them from the opposite direction. Her tear-filled eyes looked up at them with a curious expression. She was wearing pajamas and bare feet, her face was dirty and her hair needed to be brushed. The poor thing was the picture of neglect. She picked up an old discarded coffee cup off the floor and looked inside before dropping it and kicking it across the hallway.

"Hey there, sweetheart," Jackson said, kneeling down a few feet from the girl. "Where is your mommy?"

Her big brown eyes stared up at Jackson and Teddy. She sniffed and wiped her nose before pointing down the hall. "Can you show us where she is?" Teddy held out his hand.

She looked hesitantly at Teddy's hand and then up at his bigger than life smile. Teddy had a way with people that made them trust him. Unlike Jackson and Dane, who scared more people than not, Teddy could win anyone over with no more than a simple gesture.

The little girl's face lit up and she slid her little hand into his. They followed her lead down a few doors until they came to a door that was left open. They could hear a heated argument between a man and a woman. Jackson knocked hard enough to be heard over their voices. A moment later the door swung open, revealing a woman with narrowed eyes. "What?" she barked at Jackson and Teddy. When she noticed her child, her mouth fell open in shock.

"What's going on here?" the woman gasped, grabbing for her child's hand and pulling her inside.

"Try taking care of your kid," Jackson bit off coldly. The woman scoffed at Jackson's words.

"Bye princess." Teddy waved to her. The little girl smiled and waved back before her mother slammed the door in their faces.

"You're welcome," Teddy said sarcastically. "Some people should never have children," he said in disbelief.

"Ain't that a fact," Jackson said, shaking his head. "Let's go."

Jackson knocked on room 926, placing his hand on the door frame as he waited for an answer.

"Maybe he's not home," Teddy said after a few minutes of silence on the other side of the door.

"He's home," Jackson said with certainty. He knocked again, harder this time. They waited a few more minutes before the sound of multiple door locks released in close succession. A short man, with long wayward hair and wire-framed glasses, opened the door enough to glance out in the hallway. He gave the entire hallway an entire sweep before his eyes settled on Jackson and Teddy.

"Let us the fuck in, Max. We're alone and no one is following us," Jackson said impatiently. Max pushed his glasses up his nose before stepping back and opening the door just wide enough for Jackson and Teddy to squeeze through. Once inside, Max closed the door and began to secure his multiple locks.

"You know if someone wants in those locks won't keep them out, right?" Jackson shook his head, looking at all the strange locks that Max had installed along the back of the door.

"Only two of them are actual locks. See this one?" He pointed at a red wire that was twisted through a chain. If someone breaks this wire, it triggers this little unit..." Max pointed to a canister in the corner that had some kind of box mounted to the top. "...to release a gas that will knock out even big guys like you two. Bam!" Max smacked his hands together hard. "Out like little babies." He grinned madly, showing his crooked teeth.

Jackson could see Teddy's eyes light up as he walked over to the canister. "Don't touch it," Max warned. "It's a little finicky. It's already gone off a few times and put me out. You wake up with one mother of a headache, let me tell you." Max shook his head.

The warning did nothing to deter Teddy, who was leaning over the unit examining the setup of the gas discharging device.

"If that thing goes off, Teddy, you better fucking hold your breath, because I'm not dragging your ass out of here," Jackson warned. Teddy only ignored him and continued his exploration. Anything mechanical was like drugs to an addict for Teddy. He needed to know how everything worked, even if it meant pulling it apart and putting it back together piece by piece.

Max's apartment was a stark contrast to the dingy interior of the building. His apartment was spotless and smelled of bleach and pine. Max ran an unofficial crime and trauma scene decontamination company and his cleanliness didn't stop with his job. Every inch of his apartment was sterile and resembled more of an operating room than a home. The entire room was bare, with minimal furniture except for a large wall of computers, and electronics that put Jackson's simple laptop to shame.

Max not only made bodies disappear without a trace, he was also in the business of knowing important information that people paid significantly for. Jackson had come to know Max when he had ran in Black's circle on the streets before Giles had pulled him from this life and directed him toward earning a badge. Black was a drug trafficker on the streets of Belhaven and had been before Jackson had started testing the other side of the waters when he was only thirteen years old. Jackson found his way into his circle when he met Nate, a fellow orphan that foster care dumped into a home that was scarier than the streets. Nate had brought Jackson into Black's fold shortly after they had met.

At first Jackson couldn't believe his good fortune. Black's organization seemed like the greatest thing his young mind could fathom. He felt empowered by the connections and the rewards the life offered until he discovered how Black rose to power. Black's men dealt on street corners, snatching the scraps John Stodden tossed away. While Stodden ran his empire with the elite of Belhaven, Black ran it from the bowels of the city. Jackson's life became darker than ever, his boundaries pushed so far he knew there was no going back no matter how many oaths he now took to uphold the law.

Max had a twisted view of the world but Jackson knew he would never intentionally hurt anyone. Jackson had earned Max's trust long ago and Max knew that Jackson's badge didn't change the person he was. They had a trust that had never swayed over the years and didn't pass judgment on one another. They both knew how warped life had made them and they understood each other. Max would give Jackson the truth and never led him astray.

Jackson looked up at the multiple screens Max

had positioned on the two large desks placed side-by-side. One of the screens showed a woman in the shower, lathering soap in her hair. The angle of the camera was positioned perfectly to capture her entire figure.

"What's this?" Teddy asked, pointing at the woman.

Max looked up at the screen with a smile. "Room 404." He wiggled his brows. "She's got sweet tits."

"I can see that. Why is her shower under your surveillance?" Teddy asked, trying to avoid looking at the naked woman who had no idea she was being watched as she washed herself.

"I like to know what's going on in the building. Did you bring the cash?" Max asked Jackson.

Jackson slipped the bag off his shoulder and set it on Max's desk. "Ten for our previous arrangement and five for today, just like we agreed," Jackson said as he pulled the zipper open and revealed the cash.

"Do I even want to know about this previous arrangement?" Teddy asked with raised brows.

"No," Jackson and Max said in unison.

Teddy shrugged his shoulders nonchalantly before he pressed the power button on the monitor with the woman in the shower. "I feel like a rapist watching that shit, man. It's fucking wrong."

"Your little cop friend isn't gonna get all righteous on me and start wielding his badge, is he?" Max narrowed his eyes on Teddy.

"No man, relax," Jackson assured him. "We don't have a problem as long as you keep your hands off."

"No problem. I get my thrills from watching," Max said, flipping the screen back on and observing the woman without shame as she stepped out of the shower and grabbed a towel before he turned back to Jackson and Teddy. "My rates will be going up if you have me running all the way to little shit towns like Freyview. That place is too small to show up on a fucking map."

"When this is all over I won't have a reason to go back," Jackson assured him. "What do you have for me?"

Max grabbed a piece of paper off his desk. "Word on the street is that Stodden's had a hotel owner in Sugar Hill stretched over the coals about owing him money and then all of a sudden the problem seemed to go away. Based on my source, no money exchanged hands because the hotel is going under massive renovations and there's no cash to pay off such a hefty dept."

"They must have reached some kind of agreement," Jackson said with a thoughtful frown.

"Yeah, there's also word that Stodden partnered with a man named Brian Crothers. They're building a private club called "Bitter Sweet." It's due to open in a month. It might also be a place to hide something you don't want found. That's all I could find. That man's shit is locked up tighter than a fucking bank."

"Okay, we can work with that. What about the guns?'

"Yeah." Max picked up a stack of cards sitting on his desk and shuffled through them. "Here it is."

Max passed Jackson a card for an Italian eatery a few blocks away.

"Bella Italia?" Jackson questioned.

"*That,* my friend, is your weapon supply. Anything you need these guys can hook you up, no questions asked. I've a few references that swear by them."

"Who's their supplier?"

"The guns come in the fucking shipyard with their bread, pasta, and whatever the fuck else they serve at Italian restaurants. The supervisor who oversees the merchandise is Macario Aiello's son-in-law, the owner of the restaurant. It's a pretty tight operation. They haven't had anyone sniff around on their tail yet. On the back of the card is the name of the guy who will set up the meeting. He deals with Aiello on a regular basis and he owes me a favor."

Jackson flipped the card over. The name **"Steven"** was written next to a number.

Max pulled open his desk drawer and picked up a manila envelope. "Here you are," Max said, passing Jackson the envelope. Jackson opened it up to reveal three fake IDs for him, Teddy, and Dane.

"Aiello is pretty thorough, just be sure you leave your badges at home. The IDs should be good enough to make the exchange. He'll want some credentials before he makes the sale to make sure you ain't cops." Max chuckled. "Your cop friends better not tear this shit down on me. If anyone finds out I lead cops into this place, I'm as good as dead."

"It won't come back on you, Max. I'll make sure of it," Jackson assured.

"Steven's word should be enough of a resume.

He's been in a working relationship with Aiello for a few years now. Once you stack your armory, what's the plan with Stodden?" Max asked curiously.

"We're going to blow him the fuck up," Jackson said confidently.

"Oh shit." Max smiled. "I always liked your style, Jackson. "Steven already has your names. Just call him up and he'll take care of the arrangements."

Jackson nodded. "Thanks, man."

"You know Stodden's got a hit out on you?" Max asked.

"I know." Jackson held out his hand to Max. "See you later, Max."

Max took his hand in a firm shake. "Good luck, old friend."

"Leave that woman alone," Teddy warned over his shoulder as he headed toward the door, leaving Max in front of his computers.

As soon as the elevator doors closed, Teddy turned toward Jackson. "You know if I had a conscience, I would try to talk you out of all this shit. We keep digging deeper and deeper, eventually the walls will cave in on us. You know that, right?"

"Yes," Jackson replied.

Teddy hit number four on the elevator.

"Really?" Jackson threw Teddy a look. "We don't have time."

"I'll only be a minute. You know I can't leave that shit alone," Teddy said, searching Jackson's expression for understanding.

"Hurry up. I'll hold the elevator."

"Thanks, man," Teddy said as he darted out the

41

opening doors. Jackson leaned against the door to keep the elevator open. He watched Teddy walk a few doors down until he reached number 404. Jackson sighed and pulled out his phone. He brought up his favorite picture of Lexie. She was wearing only her lacy white underwear as the late afternoon sun cast its glow on her skin. The look in her eyes and the smile upon her face made his chest ache. It was the moment before she dove into the water, the moment he realized she was about to turn him inside out and he couldn't do anything to stop it.

He wondered when everything had shifted and his sole focus became saving Lexie. The case that had haunted him for years had taken a backseat to her safety. Looking at her image, it pained him to think that something happened to her while he was trying to be smart about playing his cards. He couldn't afford to be reckless when approaching John Stodden or he could cost all of them their lives.

If he closed his eyes tight and thought of her, he could almost smell her soft floral scent, taste her strawberry flavored lips and feel her soft skin beneath his fingertips. He wondered if she affected him so much because she represented a beauty he had been denied his entire life. She made him desperate to be capable of love, he wanted to give her everything but he was a shadow next to her bright light.

Jackson's attention snapped back into focus when he heard a door close. He looked up to see Teddy heading back toward him. His seemed a little rattled as he stalked toward the elevator. "What's up?" Jackson called.

"Nothing, all good," Teddy said, opening his hand to reveal a small, black camera.

"It took you long enough. What'd you say to convince her to let you in, anyway?"

Teddy flashed him a smile. "You doubt my skills. I'm offended." Teddy placed his hand against his heart.

Jackson put it from mind. "Let's get going." He pressed the ground floor button and they watched the doors close.

"Did you know that after my sister was found, a witness came forward and placed her at the park the afternoon she went missing?" Teddy said thoughtfully. Jackson shook his head when Jackson looked at him. "The witness said a man approached her and it wasn't long before she walked off with him. I think about that all the time…" Teddy wiped his hands down his face. "What the fuck could he have said to her to make her leave with him?" Teddy sighed. "The description of the man and his vehicle brought the cops to the doorstep of a man named Peter Wilson. Despite the evidence, he was dismissed as a suspect because he had a solid alibi. The man who gave him his free pass was none other than John Stodden, who confirmed that Peter could not have been at the park that day. The case against Wilson was dropped immediately and the other man was suddenly accused. He didn't fit the description of the suspect, but it didn't matter. The case was closed and filed away and we were all supposed to move on."

"I didn't know, man," Jackson said, understanding the sorrow seeping from his friend.

"Do you think that Giles let us off the leash because he knows that this is exactly what we would do? I know he doesn't believe for one second that we wouldn't cross the line to take this fucker down."

"Makes sense," Jackson said thoughtfully.

"If we get caught he won't be able to let us get away with it, though. He's too good of a cop for that."

"I know, but I won't let you go down for this shit. I promise, Ted."

"I'm not scared of getting caught, Jackson. I'm scared our plan won't work," Teddy said solemnly.

"It'll work."

The elevator doors opened and Jackson saw Dane across the lobby, sitting on an old torn sofa. He was leaning back with his hands behind his head. The two women that had been lingering in the entrance were sitting on either side, leaned over his lap as they kissed and fondled each other.

CHAPTER FIVE

Stephanie

Stephanie heard soft humming, but when she tried to concentrate on the sound to determine where it was coming from it seemed to fade away like a distant memory. She didn't know if it was her imagination or if she had fallen asleep and hadn't realized it. He lifted her head off the thin pillow and looked around the dark room, confirming she was still alone and surrounded by the thick smell of death.

Stephanie tried to hold onto the hope that she would be free of this place, but the long stretches of time picked away at her and she couldn't help but feel desolated at her situation. She could hear the whispers of defeat when she closed her eyes and see the faces of all the people she loved become blurred behind the fear that was her constant companion.

Stephanie pulled the thin blanket tighter around her shoulders and tried to stay the chill that pulled at her bones. She tried to imagine being anywhere else, but reality would not let her escape the truth. She flipped on her back and looked up at the ceiling. If she stared long enough, the shadows seemed to shift and move around the ceiling as if spectators were watching her. Stephanie strained to envision the feeling of the sun against her skin, warming her.

The sound of humming found her again. It was a soft feminine voice that seemed out of place in these dark walls. The sound stopped suddenly when Stephanie opened her eyes to realize it was her voice. The tune seemed so familiar, like an old memory she was trying to recall, but it remained just out of reach.

Stephanie turned on her side and grabbed a hold of the side of the mattress to keep herself grounded. Her mind played so many tricks on her and she was having a hard time distinguishing between her dreams and reality as she drifted in and out of sleep. Her fingers dipped into the side of the mattress as the material gave way. She sat up and looked over the edge to see a hole in the side. Stephanie slipped her fingers inside to feel the soft material that made the core of the mattress until her fingers brushed against something hard. She dug in further until she could grasp a small, hard object.

Stephanie held it up to the dim light. It was a ring, and from the look of the size and style, it was a woman's wedding band. She slipped it on her ring finger and felt a tear escape her. She knew she was not the first to be locked in these walls, but finding a belonging of another that had gone through this same fate brought her so much sadness. She wondered if the husband of this woman was still searching for her somewhere or maybe he thought she had left him without a word.

Stephanie slipped the ring from her finger and tucked it back deep inside the mattress so *he* would not find it. She knew it was probably the one thing of hers he did not destroy and she wanted to make sure it remained safe. Strangely, it made her feel a little less alone.

Her teeth chattered uncontrollably as she curled herself up in a tight ball, wondering if she would lose her sanity or her life first. She placed her hand over the mattress where the ring was tucked safely away and wept for herself and the others she feared never made it out of this hell.

CHAPTER SIX

Jackson

"What'd we find out?" Dane asked as he crawled into the back of Jackson's car with a groan of discomfort.

"We confirmed Max is a sick motherfucker," Teddy said through clenched teeth. He pushed his seat back once Dane was in back and slid into the front. He pulled his phone out of his pocket and dialed a number. Teddy was sensitive to the mistreatment of women. It was the one thing that turned his usually playful mood upside down. Jackson knew Teddy would not be able to shake off what he saw. "Evan's not answering." Teddy ended the call.

"He's probably sleeping or crying," Jackson said without concern. Evan had been trying to wean himself off the drugs, making him a complete head case. It had been a painful week and Jackson's patience was thin. "He needs a fucking rehab facility."

"I get shot and you guys try to fucking replace me with a junkie," Dane said with a shake of his head.

"And now we're stuck with two whiny invalids." Teddy rolled his eyes.

"Serves you right," Dane said.

This protective side of Teddy surprised most people because Teddy cycled through women like he did clothes. Teddy always made sure his intentions were clear before he took a woman to bed. He never led them to believe that it was more than just sex, but even spelling it out never stopped the few wishful believers that they had the power to change his outlook on relationships.

"How much did you have to pay for that little show we walked in on?" Jackson asked, looking at Dane in the rear view mirror as he pulled out of the parking lot.

A smile swallowed Dane's face, the lingering look of pain vanished. "Ten bucks," he said proudly. "It's all I had on me and they didn't complain. I was a little weary at first, those girls have been ridden hard and put away wet, but when they started kissing...I wasn't complaining. Best ten dollars I ever spent." Dane leaned back, stretching out his big frame in the small backseat. "Max give you the info we need?"

"Yeah, we have a couple of good leads for his whereabouts and the contact to set up the hardware hookup."

"Fuck yeah." Dane rubbed his hands together excitedly. "I can't wait to start blowing shit up. Hear from Giles yet or is he still giving you breathing room?"

"He checked in. I told him we're finishing up some loose ends in Belhaven and then we needed a few personal days to burn off some steam," Jackson said, tapping his steering wheel mindlessly.

"Did he seem to buy it?" Dane asked.

"He didn't ask any questions." Jackson frowned.

"Giles didn't ask any questions? That in itself is a red flag. I think he knows exactly what we're up to," Teddy added.

"Did you tell Giles about what Mary said about Rosh?" Dane questioned. The very accusation was hard to swallow that Rosh was behind his father's murder, but the more Jackson thought about it, the more he realized he could not deny the possibility. Before he could bring this to Giles, he needed irrefutable evidence because Rosh and Giles were close personally and professionally. He couldn't swing that accusation around without weight behind it.

"I need evidence first." Jackson shook his head.

"It's hard to believe," Teddy said. "Rosh has a lot of credence in both Oxford and Belhaven districts. If he's in bed with Stodden…"

"We have company," Jackson said when he noticed a black car on their tail.

Both Teddy and Dane turned in their seats. "Stodden really wants us out of the picture, doesn't he?" Teddy said, pulling his piece from his holster.

"I'm gonna lose him. Hold on back there, Dane," Jackson said as he stepped on the gas.

"Go for it," Dane said, his gun already in hand. Jackson took a sharp right and headed down a less populated street. He could hear Dane groan in pain from the abrupt turns but it couldn't be helped. The price John put on their heads brought out the big guns and these men would not think twice before putting a bullet in their heads.

"We need to find a new ride, Jackson. There aren't that many BMW M4s on the street with the fucking side ripped off them," Teddy said, looking in the side view mirror.

"Yeah, yeah. I changed the plates at least," Jackson said distractedly. He knew this city well enough to know which area he would be able to get an advantage in a chase. He also needed to avoid the police. Their plan would only work if they stayed off the radar, they needed to remain invisible. He sped up and ramped off the main road to an underpass. The pursuing car was quick on their heels as it followed them to an industrial part of the city.

"Shit." Jackson slammed on the brakes when he turned the corner and narrowly missed the barricade in a construction area, coming dangerously close to a few workers directing traffic. Dane hit the back of Teddy's seat.

"Fuck me," Dane whimpered as he tried to right himself back on the seat.

"Put your fucking belt on!" Teddy shook his head.

Once the man holding the stop sign thawed from the shock, he started yelling profanities and waving his hands at their vehicle. Teddy gave the angry worker a friendly wave as Jackson threw the car into reverse and swerved around the black car that came barreling around the corner. The workers ran out of the way and Jackson avoided the other car as he took off in the opposite direction.

Jackson headed toward a few abandoned building by the shipyards. The approaching car released a few rounds, clipping the side of Jackson's car.

"Jesus Christ." Jackson swerved before he sped through a parking lot and headed around back of a large metal building. "I'm gonna need some fancy gun work, Dane. I need this fucker off my ass," Jackson said as the black sedan appeared in his rear view mirror again.

"It's kinda hard when your back windows don't open," Dane complained, tapping his gun against the glass.

"Here." Teddy pulled his seat forward as far as he could and collapsed the back forward against him. Dane leaned on the back of the seat and managed to angle himself to get his arm out the window. Dane twisted around in his seat, aiming his gun toward the chasing car.

"Hurry the fuck up. You're heavy as shit," Teddy complained as Dane pushed his weight against him, shoving him into the dash.

"Hold on." Jackson made a quick right between two buildings, avoiding large trash bins lined up along the side of the building.

"Jesus," Dane cried out. "I won't be able to shoot anything if you don't stop tossing me around."

"I can't help it, this fucker can drive," Jackson said.

Dane shot off two rounds, blowing out the two

front tires of the car. It swerved before colliding with the side of the building. Jackson slowed down and turned around to get a visual. The damage on the front end of the car was extensive but Jackson didn't stick around to see the condition of the men in the car as he sped off.

***

Jackson pulled the car to a stop in front of a rundown looking motel. The color of the building was a strange shade of salmon, dirtied from years of weather. Mint green shutters lined every window on the two story building with the occasional one missing. The whole building needed a fresh coat of paint to make it more welcoming but it served its purpose.

"I'm going to call and set up our meeting." Jackson held up the card Max had given him. "I'll be right in."

"Sounds good," Teddy said, stepping out of the car. "We'll go make sure Evan's still alive."

Dane took a few minutes to climb out of the back of the car. Jackson's driving did nothing to help his injuries and he was looking a little pale. "You gonna be all right, man?" Jackson asked.

"Just need a beer." Dane threw him a smile before he climbed out of the backseat.

He shut the door and followed Teddy up the metal stairwell to the second story.

Jackson grabbed his phone out of the glovebox and dialed the number on the back of the card.

"Yeah?" someone answered after two rings.

"Steven?"

"The very one."

"It's Jackson."

"When do you want me to set it up?" Steven asked, jumping straight to business.

"ASAP."

"I'll get back to you," Steven said before disconnecting the call.

Jackson rubbed the side of his face, taking a deep breath as he leaned back against his seat. He reached over and opened the glovebox and pulled out Lexie's purse. He took out the diary he had found the day he collected it from the diner. He had read every word Lexie's mother wrote. He opened to the entry that he had read over and over.

August 27

I can't sleep because every time I close my eyes I see that night replay over and over. I can't escape it.

I've been hiding in a motel for the last week. I don't even know where I am. I drove in a complete daze, unable to read the road signs. I can't even bring myself to write what happened. I'm scared to write the words.

When I think of my baby I know I would do it all again, but my only regret is that I didn't figure out who Officer Finley's partner was sooner. I could have stopped it from happening and he might still be alive.

Officer Finley was the only officer who didn't give up on finding the girl with the rose tattoo. I now fear that his death also means that she will now remain missing. No one will look for her and bring her home.

I keep thinking about his family. He mentioned he had a young son. It breaks my heart knowing his little boy will never know the man his father was.

Jackson closed his eyes and leaned his head back against the head rest. If Rosh was his father's murderer, he needed the evidence Mary mentioned. Rosh was a decorated officer that was respected among all his peers. If he did what Mary Connor accused him of, Jackson would make sure that he was stripped and exposed for what he really was. Jackson wanted revenge. His thirst for it had driven him his entire life and he would seek it until his last breath.

Jackson opened his eyes when he heard someone tap on his window. Teddy was leaning against his car. He tucked the diary away and opened the door. "What's up?" he said, stepping out of the car and noticing Teddy's expression.

"He's not here," Teddy said, throwing his hand in the air.

"Fuck," Jackson breathed out in frustration. He slammed his door and headed up the steps toward Evan's room.

Jackson swung the door open to see the blankets

ripped off the bed and Evan's things scattered on the floor. He looked up at Dane, who was holding up a piece of paper. "Who's Seth?"

"Oh shit." Jackson raked his hands through his hair. "He's an asshole from my past that has the worst fucking timing," Jackson bit off.

"He can't spell for shit, either," Dane said, passing him the paper.

CHAPTER SEVEN

Lexie

Lexie felt something brush softly against her cheek, a whisper of a touch that barely roused her sleepy mind. She shifted and opened her eyes, realizing that against her best intentions she had fallen asleep. She jolted awake when she noticed someone standing in front of her. A surprised gasp spilled from her as she looked up into Flint's eyes.

Lexie pushed herself as far back in the chair as she could. She was angry with herself for falling asleep and allowing someone to enter her room without her knowledge, especially with the way Flint looked at her. He seemed completely at ease staring at her like he was slowly peeling away her layers. She wondered what was going on in his dark mind as he watched her squirm uneasily.

Flint seemed to have a close relationship with madness that made fear spin through her blood. He was unpredictable and in some ways appeared to be more dangerous than John. While John was cold and calculating, Flint seemed more prone to tap into his animalistic nature.

"What are you doing in here?" Lexie asked as she scanned the room to see what else she possibly missed as she slept. For days she tried to remain alert to her surroundings, sleeping for short intervals or not at all, but she realized exhaustion finally claimed her. She allowed herself to be vulnerable, something she promised herself she wouldn't do.

Her room barely resembled the beautifully decorated space it was when she was first brought here. After she had talked to John that first night when she had mentioned the camera and he had responded using camera in the plural sense, it was not missed on her. The first thing she did when they brought her back to her room was tear it apart looking for more cameras. After moving furniture and pulling paintings off the walls, she finally found what she was looking for. A camera pointed directly toward her bed. She didn't trust John when he said they were inactive. She wasn't going to take the risk, flushing all the components down the toilet. She wanted no trace left behind.

"I see you didn't like your gift," Flint said, frowning as he looked at the remains of the camera scattered on the floor. The television was leaning against the front of the entertainment unit with the screen completely destroyed.

"It's wasn't the camera I have an issue with. It's who gave it to me," Lexie said sadly, looking at the expensive piece of equipment she demolished, but she knew she could never look through the lens without thinking of John.

"John wants to see you," Flint said as he walked over to her closet, stepping over debris.

Lexie pushed herself off the chair. "Why? Is it about the test results?" She had been dreading the moment that John would hear back about the paternity test. She was absolutely terrified about what it meant to be related to him and just as scared to find out what would happen to her if she wasn't. She was still no further in trying to formulate an escape plan because John kept her locked away without any unnecessary contact with anyone.

Flint nodded his head. The confirmation made a wave of nausea hit her hard and she grabbed hold of the arm of the chair for support. She watched quietly as Flint shuffled through her dresses before selecting a soft blue one. She was completely speechless with the realization she would soon find out the answer to the question in her mother's diary. Would she be the daughter of the man her mother hated or the man she loved?

"You should wear this. It's the same color as your eyes." He laid it out on the bed and ran his fingers over the fabric before his eyes found her.

"Can you take me to see my mother?" Lexie asked as a swell of emotion filled her chest.

"No," Flint responded coldly.

"Why? I just need to see her for a moment," Lexie begged as she rounded the bed. She hoped there was a part of him that was human enough to understand her plea. "I need to see her, please." Lexie wrapped her fingers around his forearm. She hated the fact that she was trying to find a connection with a man that made her skin crawl, but she was desperate to sway someone to her side. She was not naïve to the way he looked at her. She could see the excitement flare in his eyes when he looked at her hand upon his arm so she decided to take advantage of his attraction to her. She was backed into a corner and would use any angle she had.

"It's John's call when you see your mother, but I may be able to convince him," Flint said, looking deep into Lexie's eyes. It made a cold shiver rake through her body, but she tried to mask it by running her hand along his arm.

"Thank you, Flint."

"You should get dressed," Flint said, walking over to her dresser and sliding the top drawer open. Lexie watched him run his fingers over the rows of underwear before selecting a lacy white thong and matching bra. "I've always liked white. It's so pure," Flint said, running his finger over the lace detail. He set them on the bed next to the dress. "Change, Lexie." He nodded toward the clothes.

Lexie looked down at her night dress and then back at him. "Here?"

"Yes," Flint responded with a tone that made her realize his intentions. "I want to see you...all of you."

Lexie knew Flint would not make this easy because he was not a man that would play nicely. She wanted to run away from him. Every part of her wanted to shove him and make a run for the door, but she knew she wouldn't get far. If she was going to survive this hell she was going to have to get her hands dirty. Lexie tried to ignore his sickening gaze as she grabbed the hem of her night shirt and took a deep breath. Her stomach felt like a hard ball that threatened to explode in a wave of nausea but she needed to reel in her emotions. She needed to harden her shell and force herself to move.

Lexie slowly pulled the oversized sleep shirt up her body and over her head. She was standing in front of him with only her panties and bra. Normally she would sleep without either, but being in this place, she was unwilling to get too comfortable.

"Look at me," Flint said, his voice sounded raw and terrifying. "Look at me when you take off your underwear."

Lexie looked up into his dark eyes, his arms crossed over his chest. She could feel her hands shaking as she reached around her back and unclasped her bra. Every muscle in her body was tensed and ready to flee should he approach. She would not let him touch her without a fight. She slipped the straps from her shoulders and let the material slide down her arms. Lexie set it on the bed and picked up the white bra.

He didn't try to hide his obvious desire for her as it strained against his pants. "Take off your underwear first," Flint demanded.

Lexie let the material of the bra slip through her fingers and dropped it back on the bed. She tried to let her mind wander from the situation at hand so she could get through this. Her thoughts found Jackson, his image filled her mind. She desperately sought to remember the feeling of elation she had felt in his arms. Despite the fact that he had

61

deceived her, what she had felt in those moments was real to her. Then thoughts of Alex quickly followed and she found anger burning through her other emotions because her heart hadn't found his memory first when she needed comfort. She was no better than Jackson. She had betrayed Alex and he was far more deserving of loyalty than she was.

"Slowly," Flints said, lowering his hand to his erection pulsing against his pants.

Lexie bit her tongue, distracting her mind with pain instead. She slid her fingers under the material of her underwear and slid them down her legs, until they dropped to the floor.

"Turn around."

Lexie took a deep breath and forced herself not to cover herself with her arms as she slowly spun around, trying not to look as terrified as she felt. Her play toward his desires would not work if she allowed him to see how she really felt. It was taking all her energy to make her expression not reflect the emotions that brewed inside her.

"Does John know you're here?" Lexie asked, trying to make her voice project confidence.

His eyes snapped to hers and she almost thought she saw a flash of fear. "I'll leave you to finish getting ready and come back for you shortly," Flint announced before he left. Once Lexie heard the door close and the lock engage, she grabbed her underwear and frantically pulled them on. Tears flooded her eyes but she made no attempt to hide her feelings now that she was alone. She needed to release all the pent up emotion. She hated Flint for making her feel the way he did and she hoped eventually she could turn the tables.

Lexie pulled her dress over her head and darted into the bathroom to wash her face. She needed to scrub away her tears and ready herself to face John and the truth of who her father was. Lexie grabbed a towel off the counter and dried her face. Looking in the mirror, she squared her shoulders. "I will not break. I will be strong."

Lexie put on a fresh face of makeup, covering the dark circles under her eyes, and searched through the lipsticks, hoping to find one labeled "Fuck you, John Stodden, and all your demented minions." She gave up looking at the names and just grabbed one. She ran the color across her lips and was satisfied. She looked put together enough to hide the fear lingering so close under the surface of her skin. This was the first chance she had the opportunity to leave her room since the first day and she was going to take full advantage.

True to his word, Flint returned only moments after she finished getting ready. He walked into her room without any warning. "You look lovely," Flint said, his eyes skimming her curves. Despite the fact that she was now dressed, she still felt completely exposed.

"Thank you," Lexie said politely.

"John is waiting." Flint offered his arm. Lexie forced a smile and took it. The only way she managed to hold the smile upon her face was envisioning clawing his eyes out with her fingernails.

***

"Sit." John held out his hand toward a club chair facing an ornate wooden desk. The room was a large suite consisting of multiple rooms. The décor was similar to her room but this one was more luxurious with extra attention to detail. Double doors leading into the bedroom were left open to reveal a large poster bed. Another door that led off the main area was closed and Lexie could only assume it led to another bedroom.

Lexie sat her shaky legs down before someone noticed how nervous she was. John rounded the desk and took his own chair. He was dressed as immaculately as always, without a hair out of place. He picked up a cigar sitting on an ashtray and placed it in his mouth, twisting it slowly in his lips. He leaned back in his chair and reached into his pocket and pulled out a lighter. "How did you like your gift?" John asked, holding the cigar over the lighter and twisting the end over the flame.

"It's smashing. You were too kind," Lexie said tightly before she glanced at Flint, who was standing off to the side of the room. A hint of a smile played on his lips. Three other men stood around, the embodiment of intimidation, and she felt like a mess of emotion in the middle of it all.

John brought the cigar to his lips as he continued to light the end, white smoke tendrils twisting from his mouth. He flipped the lighter closed and looked at Lexie. The smell of the cigar reminded Lexie of the old man that owned the little corner bookstore near her apartment. He was always sitting outside smoking his cigar but John's smelled heartier, like a spice mixed with a woodsy scent.

"Are you planning on keeping me locked up forever?" Lexie blurted when she couldn't stand the silence any longer. John seemed completely content with his cigar as he filled the air with his rich smoke.

"No, not forever," John said. "But it is in my best interest to do so for now." John picked up an envelope on his desk. Lexie dropped her gaze to it and suddenly it was the only thing she could see.

"What's that?" Lexie asked with wide eyes.

"It's exactly what you think it is." John ran his fingers over the white envelope before he looked up at Lexie and all the air left the room. "I'll let you do the honors," John said, passing the envelope over the desk toward her. Lexie didn't move as she looked at the envelope. The rest of the room faded away. She was terrified of what it would reveal.

"Lexie," John said with warning.

Lexie took a deep breath and snapped her attention back into focus. She took the envelope and stared down at the white rectangle of paper in her hands. She could feel everyone's eyes on her, waiting for her to open it. Lexie lifted the envelope up in front of her and tore it in half, continuing to tear the remains until the pieces were too small and she let them flutter to the floor. She looked up at John defiantly but he seemed unfazed as he puffed on his cigar.

"You already know the answer, don't you?" Lexie asked suspiciously.

"Yes, I do, but it seems you are not ready to know."

"I will never be ready."

65

"We'll see," John said, holding her gaze.

"You expect me to be on my best behavior but you lock me away like an animal. If you want me to want to know if you are my father or not, then you should start showing some humanity." Lexie found herself leaning forward in her chair. She knew John could see the fire in her eyes, she had allowed her temper to flare despite her best intentions. She watched him clench his jaw as he stared down at her as if she was a bug and he was deciding whether to step on her or not. She pulled back in her chair when she realized her misstep. She needed to change her angle or he would just lock her away again and she'd be no better off. "I really just want to see my mother. I'm scared and have no idea what you're planning to do to me. I don't know this life my mother hid from me. I have no idea who you are or what any of this means." Lexie waved her arms around her.

Lexie watched the smoke curl around his lips as he released it slowly. John glanced over at Flint before he set his cigar down on the ashtray. "Maybe a change of scenery will do you some good. We're having a small event this evening. You will come and enjoy yourself."

"I don't understand. You' are letting me out?"

John leaned forward, holding Lexie's gaze with a fierce intensity. "If you do anything out of line, you will be punished. You'll be closely guarded, so don't plan anything in that pretty little head of yours." John picked up his cigar and twisted it in his fingers. "It will give you an opportunity to become acquainted with your new home."

66

"Will my mother be there?" Lexie asked hopefully.

A knock on the door grabbed everyone's attention. One of the men opened it. A suit and tie took a few steps inside the room before stopping to address John. His dark shoulder length hair was slicked back and a neck tattoo just peeked out from the collar of his shirt. "Sorry to interrupt, John, but I have a couple of urgent matters that can't wait."

John pushed back his chair and stood up. "Flint, Jacobs, and Rayner, you're with me. Miller, make sure Lexie is brought back to her room."

Lexie watched the men file out of the room after the man with the tie and she was left in the chair with the remains of the letter scattered over her feet. She looked down at the paper, leaning forward and setting her face in her hands. She didn't want to go back to that room. She couldn't stand being confined within its walls anymore. Lexie moved her feet so the pieces of paper would shake loose and not touch her. She closed her eyes and took deep breaths.

Lexie wasn't sure how much time passed when she heard someone clear their throat. She opened her eyes and saw a piece of gum held out in front of her. She sat back in the chair and looked up into the eyes of the man she assumed was Miller, the man that was supposed to bring her back to her room.

"It's all I have and you look like you need some cheering up." He managed a crooked smile. Lexie could feel a scowl form on her face. The man standing in front of her did not fit the profile of the rest of John's men. His blue eyes were sad and not tainted like all the others. "You don't like gum? It's peppermint." He raised his brow. He couldn't have been any older than herself.

Lexie took the gum from his hand. "Thank you." He looked like a boy next door who decided to slip on an all-black attire to fit in but instead it just made him stand out more. "Why are you being nice to me?"

Miller sighed and smiled knowingly, running his hand through his blond hair. "John's not so bad. In time you will see." Miller smiled encouragingly.

"Thanks for trying to cheer me up," Lexie said as she popped the piece of gum in her mouth. "You seem different from everyone else."

"I'm the new kid in town. My uncle was the man who came looking for John. My mother passed away a few months ago and left too many bills for me to handle. My uncle offered me this job to help me get out from the debt."

"I'm so sorry about your mother," Lexie said.

"Thanks. She was sick for a long time." He scratched the back of his neck, showing his discomfort. "We should get you to your room," he said, changing the subject.

Lexie pushed herself out of the chair and stepped over the pieces of paper. She followed Miller out into the hallway. A robust looking man with a full beard approached in the opposite direction in the hallway, followed by three women dressed in revealing evening attire and heavy makeup. The first girl with curled hair and leopard print shoes narrowed her eyes when she noticed Lexie. The man stopped to open a door and the girls filed in behind him.

Lexie couldn't help but notice the apprehension on the last girl's face. She looked scared under all that glitter eyeshadow. Lexie tried to see inside the room but the man closed the door behind them. "Who are they?" Lexie asked curiously, looking back at the now closed door.

"They're here for the party tonight," Miller said casually.

"Oh...do you know where they're keeping my mother?" Lexie asked on a whim. Miller turned around and looked at Lexie. "I just want to know if she's all right. Maybe you can just show me...please."

"Lexie...I can't." Miller shook his head.

"Please. I won't say anything. Just show me where she is."

Miller looked up and down the hallway, looking tormented as he dropped his shoulders. "I can show you where but I don't have the key."

"Thank you so much," Lexie said in a rush.

He walked past the elevators toward a room down another hallway. He came to a stop in front of an unnumbered door and gave a slight nod.

Lexie walked up to the door and pressed her hand against. "Mom?" she whispered. When there was no response, she spoke a little louder. "Mom?"

"Lexie," her mother's voice answered from the other side of the door. "Are you all right, baby?"

Tears filled Lexie's eyes. "Yes, what about you?"

"Don't worry about me, Lex. How are you here?"

"I don't have long. I have to go back to my room." Lexie ran her hand over the door.

"Do you remember the girl from my diary? The one I mentioned with the rose tattoo that was taken?"

"Yes."

"The man who took her...I saw him, Lexie. You need to make sure you stay far away from him."

"Who is he?" Lexie asked.

"I don't know his name but I recognized him as soon as I saw him. He has a scar down the side of his neck."

"Okay. I'll make sure to stay away from him." Lexie stared at her hand spread out against the door. "John knows...he knows if I'm his daughter or not. I'm scared."

"Oh Lexie. I'm so sorry this is happening to you. I tried to protect you..."

A hand was clamped over Lexie's mouth and she was hauled backwards into a room on the other side of the hallway. "Quiet," Miller whispered in her ear as he pushed her against the wall. She nodded her head and listened quietly as footsteps approached in the hallway.

"All clear," a man called out in the hall before his footsteps faded off. Miller stayed close to the door for a few minutes as Lexie tried to calm her racing heart. The room they were in was stripped bare and looked as if it was recently painted. She had so much more to say to her mother but she knew Miller would not risk it again.

She didn't protest when he grabbed her by the shoulder and led her out into the hallway. They walked past her mother's door and she couldn't look away. Talking to her mother through a door wasn't enough. She needed to see her and wrap her arms around her.

Miller led them onto the elevator, and once the doors closed, she noticed him visibly relax.

"Thank you," Lexie whispered.

"Yeah," Miller said tightly as he pressed the button for her floor and avoided eye contact. Lexie wrapped her arms around herself and followed him numbly as he led her back to her room.

CHAPTER EIGHT

Jackson

Jackson pulled off a dirt road into the driveway of an old farm. The house and barn were nestled on an overgrown property that ran against a heavily wooded area on the outskirts of Belhaven. Jackson parked his car in front of the white house. It had an oversized front porch with a broken swing that hung haphazardly from one chain. The property was a ghost of the quaint family home it would have been before it was left to the elements. It was the address Seth had left in Evan's motel room.

Two men leaned against a black sedan. They both wore oversized t-shirts and torn jeans and looked completely out of place in their surroundings. The man with a flat-brimmed ball hat pulled out a piece he had tucked in his belt. He held the gun by his side in warning as he rested his elbow on the car. The other pulled a long drag from his cigarette and watched them through narrow eyes.

"Do you want to keep your broken ass in the car, Dane?" Teddy asked as he grabbed the handle of the door.

"Fuck no, let me out." Dane hit the back of Teddy's seat impatiently.

"Fine, let's go save my baby brother." Teddy chuckled.

Jackson opened his door and stepped out into the sunny afternoon. The heat felt good on his neck as he surveyed the lot. The two men were the only bodies manning the exterior. Jackson swung his door closed and ran his fingers along the scraped body of his car. He had been too distracted to deal with the damage. Teddy was right; it was like having a target painted on their backs.

"We're looking for Seth," Jackson said as he approached the two men.

"Who's asking?" The one with the cigarette tossed the butt on the ground toward Jackson's feet with an insolent smile on his face. Jackson clenched his teeth irritably. He never had much tolerance for the idiots Seth kept in his circle. They smoked more crack than they sold and took stupid risks, thinking they were invincible. It looked like nothing had changed in the last ten years. It may have been new faces but it was the same ignorance.

"Tell him Jackson is here."

"You the dirty cop?" he asked as he tilted his chin and pulled out his box of cigarettes.

Jackson knocked them out of his hand. "Do as you're told, shit-head."

The guy watched his cigarettes scatter over the ground as they rolled out of the package. "What the

73

fuck?"

Jackson swung, his fist connected with the guy's throat. His victim's eyes bulged as he grabbed at his neck. He struggled to breathe, falling back against the car.

"Don't move," Dane threatened. Dane had his gun pointed at the man's forehead before he even realized it. His panicked gaze flickered between Jackson and Dane. "Go tell Seth we're here." Jackson waved his hand toward the door impatiently.

The guy shuffled his feet nervously, glancing at his friend who was recovering from Jackson's hit, before he took off toward the door and disappeared inside.

The front door opened a moment later and a man stepped out that Jackson had hoped to never see again, Seth Marshall. He wore a short-sleeve plaid shirt partially tucked into his low riding jeans. Three armed men filed out behind him, two of whom Jackson recognized from years ago, looking the same as the day he left. Seth stopped on the top step and pulled a cigarette from his pocket and lit it. Jackson noticed he was missing the baby and ring fingers on his left hand.

"It's been a long time, Jacks," Seth said coldly.

"Not long enough," Jackson responded with the same lack of affection. "Where is he?"

"He's here," Seth confirmed with a cool confidence as he walked down the porch steps. "I heard you were back in town dirtying that shiny badge of yours."

Jackson had known that picking up those drugs

for Evan was going to put him on the radar. He just didn't know it would be Seth that would be sniffing around.

"What the fuck do you want, Seth?" Jackson asked. "I don't have time for your games."

The front door of the house opened and Jackson got the surprise of his life. Nate. He was the one person Jackson had considered a friend all those years ago. He looked thinner than he remembered with an unhealthy tone to his skin, but it was unmistakeably him. As soon as he saw Nate, Jackson put the pieces together. Jackson looked back at Seth, who had a satisfied grin on his face, but Nate refused to look him in the eye.

"So tell me, why did Black let you live?" Jackson asked. He knew Nate had sold him out as the person who had revealed Seth's indiscretions behind Black's back. Anyone who crossed Black ended up dead, no questions asked, which begged the question as to why Seth was still living and breathing.

"We came to an agreement."

"Was that part of the agreement?" Jackson nodded toward Seth's mutilated hand.

Seth lifted up his hand and studied the remaining fingers with a frown. "Black always favored the blade over a gun. Luckily we came to terms and it seems we had a mutual enemy that ran away and hid behind a badge and eventually got one of his very own. You should have stayed on the other side, Jackson."

"And miss out on this?" Jackson held his arms out beside him.

"Who are your friends?" Seth asked, eyeing Teddy and Dane flanking Jackson.

"Oh how rude of me. Let me introduce you." Jackson waved toward Teddy. "This is *Fuck...*" Then waved toward Dane. "And *You*. Now give us our guy."

Seth laughed and shook his head. "I always liked you, Jackson. Too bad things turned out the way they did."

"I'm heartbroken, really," Jackson said with a bored tone.

Jackson knew exactly what Seth's plan was. He did not plan to let any of them leave alive. Seth was as reckless as they came, which was why after fifteen years wielding what little power he had over his men he was still only one step above them.

Seth took a long drag on his cigarette. "I knew it was only a matter of time before you came crawling back."

"Well, congratulations, Seth. Is this the part where you start to bitch about what happened ten years ago?"

"Check them for weapons." Seth nodded toward a few of his men. They stepped forward and patted them down, disarming them of their guns.

"All good," one of his men said, placing Dane's last gun on the hood of the car.

Seth narrowed his eyes. "Let's go for a little walk." Seth started to walk toward the barn. Jackson glanced back at Teddy and Dane to give them warning that things were about to go downhill fast before he turned and followed Seth. One of the armed men swung open the large door. It scraped along the ground as he pulled against its resistance. The voices inside the barn immediately quieted as Seth entered first.

"Your friend doesn't know when to shut up," Seth said as he waved toward Evan. He was gagged and tied to a chair. Dried blood covered his chin and stained the front of his shirt as he slumped forward in his chair.

"That's something we agree on," Jackson said as he surveyed the interior of the barn. Evan stirred at the sound of Jackson's voice.

Three men stood up from a small table tucked in the corner of the interior. They discarded their cards and picked up their guns. They walked up behind Evan, looking to Seth for orders.

Jackson walked inside the barn, closely followed by Dane and Teddy. The door swung shut behind them, closing them in with Seth and eight of his men, guns in hand.

"This doesn't look like much of a party. Where are the snacks?" Teddy asked, looking around the old barn.

Seth threw Teddy an annoyed glare before he settled on Jackson. "I want to know who leaked the info to Black." Seth pulled on his smoke.

Jackson smiled cruelly. "Let me guess. For the past ten years you've been losing sleep because you can't figure out who could have possibly ratted to Black about your little side business. Let me start by saying if you didn't keep such shady motherfuckers in your circle, you wouldn't have this problem."

Seth's nose flared angrily as he blew out a lungful of smoke. Jackson knew exactly who told

Black about his indiscretions but he wasn't about to let Seth know that it wasn't one of his men. He liked the fact he didn't know who to trust. "From the looks of some of the new faces it looks like you already tried to weed out the rat."

Seth pulled out his gun and aimed it at Evan's head. "Who the fuck was it, Jacks?" Seth hollered angrily. The veins in the side of his neck bulged. "If you don't tell me I'll start with this piece of shit and then move on to your other friends until you tell me what I want to know."

Evan made a pained sound in the back of his throat as he looked at the barrel of Seth's gun and then glanced wide-eyed at Jackson.

"Do you mind putting your smoke out? My friend here has a bad case of asthma and he's very sensitive to smoke," Jackson said, pointing over his shoulder toward Dane.

Seth took a long drag and blew the smoke out. "I don't care about your fucking friend. Tell me what I want to know."

Dane starting coughing on cue, Jackson turned around and watched Dane struggle to breathe.

"Breathe, man," Teddy said in a panic before he shoved Dane in the back, knocking him into the gunman beside them. Dane grabbed the gun from the man and pulled the trigger, shooting the gun out of Seth's hand. All of Seth's men set quickly into action, Dane took out two more before the bullets started firing around the room.

Teddy made a run for Evan, knocking his chair over and getting him out of the way of the spray of bullets. Jackson struggled, grabbed the man Dane had knocked over, and used him as a shield from the bullets aimed his way. Blood sprayed from the man's mouth as he took all the bullets meant for Jackson. He dove to the side, throwing the man's body into another, taking him out and grabbing for his gun.

Jackson pulled it from his grasp and brought the butt of the gun up into the man's face, sending him to the ground before he swung the gun around to take out another man that had ducked behind a large wooden beam with his gun aimed in their direction. Jackson shot off a round first and caught him in the throat. Blood sprayed over the beam before he collapsed on the hay covered ground.

Jackson looked around to see that Dane had already taken down the rest of the men, leaving only Seth, who seemed to be trying to scramble to his feet while searching for the gun that had been knocked out of his hand. Jackson aimed his gun toward the man out cold at his feet, pulling the trigger to ensure he would not get back up before he walked toward Seth.

Seth's arm was covered in blood from his wound. He looked frantic as Jackson approached. "We can work something out, Jacks. Come on, man." Seth raised his hand while still trying to locate his gun.

"What could you possibly do for me?" Jackson asked before clenching his jaw in hatred.

"I have connections…I'm sure there's something you need," Seth pleaded.

"Wrong, but I will let you in on a little secret." Seth stopped looking for the gun. Jackson's foot bumped into something hard. He looked down and noticed Seth's gun underneath some hay scattered over the ground. He knelt down and picked it up. "Looking for this?"

Seth looked at the gun and then back up to Jackson. "Who was it?"

Jackson passed the other gun off to Teddy and aimed Seth's gun at him. Looking down the barrel at Seth's face was more satisfying than he imagined it could be. "It was your girlfriend," Jackson said in a satisfied tone. "Guess she got tired of you fucking around on her and told Black what you were up to."

"Tina?" Seth said questioningly.

"Bingo," Jackson said as he pulled the trigger. The bullet hit Seth in the center of the forehead. His body took a moment to realize the fatal blow before his eyes glazed over and his legs gave out beneath him. He landed face first onto the ground. The interior of the barn stayed eerily quiet for a moment until Evan started complaining through his gag.

"Hold on, princess," Teddy said as he pulled the gag roughly off his head.

"Ouch. That fucking hurt," Evan complained. "Untie me so I can see if I'm shot. There were fucking bullets flying everywhere."

"Calm down. You're fine." Teddy gave him a quick once over.

"Here," Dane called out before he tossed a knife that he had taken off one of the men. It embedded in the dirt a short distance from Evan's feet.

"Jesus Christ! You guys are fucking crazy."

Teddy grabbed the blade and began cutting Evan's ties to free him from the chair. As soon as

Evan was free he scrambled to his feet. He kicked the chair and looked around at the bodies.

"See, you're all good, baby bro," Teddy teased.

"Stop calling me that," Evan snapped. "I'm pretty sure cops aren't supposed to shoot people up like this. Who the fuck gave you guys badges?" Evan wiped at the blood dried on his chin.

"We got them out of cereal boxes." Dane laughed. "We still have a few lingering on the outside." Dane nodded toward the door.

Jackson nodded as he approached, signaling for him to open the door. Teddy was close on his heels as Dane pushed the door open. Jackson had his gun ready as two men approached the barn. He fired off a few rounds and the men dropped.

"Is that it?" Jackson swung around to Teddy.

"By my count there's still one missing." Jackson walked up to the two men he had just taken out before he looked up at the house. He spun around and cleared their surroundings before he was drawn to the house. He knew who was missing…Nate. "I got this," Jackson called out over his shoulder as he made his way toward the house.

Jackson readied his gun as he walked up the front step and approached the door. He pulled the screen open and walked into the house. "Nate," Jackson called out. "I know you're in here." He cleared the front room. The coffee table was covered in beer cans and garbage. In the center of the table, a platter with pink and yellow flowers decorating the outer rim displayed a substantial stash of crack. The walls showed remnants of hanging wire from pictures that were no longer there. Jackson continued onward toward the kitchen when he heard a noise. He turned the corner with his gun aimed in the direction of the commotion when he noticed the back door swing shut. He made a run for the door in pursuit, jumping over broken dishes scattered on the kitchen floor. He shoved the door open and barrelled down the back porch steps as he noticed Nate dart around the corner.

Jackson rounded the back of the house and noticed Nate was sprawled out on the ground with Dane standing over him, his gun aimed.

"Don't shoot him," Jackson called toward Dane. Jackson walked over toward Nate. He looked terrified as he stared up at Jackson. "I didn't think you'd come back, Jackson. I was just trying to stay alive." Nate raised his hands in surrender. "I'm sorry."

"Save it," Jackson spat. "Get the fuck out of here before I change my mind."

Nate scrambled to his feet. He looked as if he was going to say something before he decided to take off toward the cars parked in the driveway.

"You think it's wise to let him go?" Dane asked as he holstered his gun.

"Probably not, but I considered him a friend once," Jackson said, staring at the settling dust.

"I like to think we're mostly still the good guys, despite the shit we get into."

"You maybe. I dance too fucking close to the line. I never know which side I'm actually on anymore."

"We're always on the same side, Jackson. Wherever you are, so am I." He patted Jackson on the shoulder and started walking toward the cars.

Teddy was sitting on the hood of Jackson's car and Evan was sitting on the ground with his head between his knees when he approached them. "What the fuck's wrong with him?" Jackson asked, walking toward the black sedan where his weapons were still sitting on the hood.

"He just needs to get laid." Teddy smiled.

"Fuck you, Ted," Evan said without looking up. Jackson walked around his car to the truck and popped it open. He grabbed a bottle of water out of the back and tossed it beside Evan. Evan looked up at the water and grabbed it, twisted off the cover, and downed the entire bottle.

"I think I solved our car troubles," Teddy said with a smile. Jackson looked over the other cars in the lot before his eyes fell on a black Dodge Charger.

"Whatever car we're taking better have four doors," Dane said, walking up beside them.

"You're in luck." Teddy walked over toward the car, opened the door, and slid inside. "The keys are in it," he called out from inside the car.

Jackson's phone rang. He pulled it from his pocket and looked at the private caller ID on the display. "Hello?"

"It's Steven. Your meeting is tonight at 9:00 p.m. at the restaurant. No street clothes or he'll turn you away at the door. I'll meet you there."

"Got it," Jackson said before he heard the call disconnect.

"Who was that?" Dane asked as soon as Jackson tucked his phone away.

"We have a date."

CHAPTER NINE

Lexie

Lexie stared at the inside of the door of her room. She wished she could open it and take back her freedom, but all she could do was hope that the next time it opened she'd find an opportunity to escape. She had spent the last few hours convincing herself her plan to use Flint was her best option and she needed to be believable for it to work. She tried to pull all her reservations deep inside and lock them away. She couldn't let fear and hatred cloud her vision. She needed to keep her mother in her sights. She had no way of knowing if anyone would come for them and she had to assume she was on her own.

When Lexie was returned to her room she decided she needed to play the part of the obedient girl John was looking for. She filled the bath and added some of the expensive looking bath products. She needed to relax and be able to gain her focus. Once her muscles began to submit to the soothing heat, her mind kicked into gear.

She picked out the most lavish dress in the closet. It was a bright red with daring lines. It took a little coaxing to pull the hidden zipper closed up the side of the dress, but when she did she was pleased with the results. It was a little tight around the bust, but it would work to her benefit.

Lexie curled her hair and pinned the sides back to give it a more finished look. She applied heavy makeup around her eyes to give her a sultry evening look that suited the bold dress and finished off her look with bright red lips to match the dress.

"Nice to meet you," Lexie had said to the stranger in the mirror. This version of herself with the determined look in her eyes was new to her. She had her feet on the ground and ready to take on the difficult road ahead. Lexie couldn't help but fear the return of the broken version of herself she had been living with since Alex had died. "Do me a favor and stick around for a while." Lexie had said before sliding the cover back on her lipstick and tossing it on the counter. "I'm gonna need you."

She now sat in a chair she had pulled over to have a clear view of the door. Someone had come into her room while she was gone earlier and cleaned the mess she had made. The pictures were rehung. The television was replaced, along with the remote that sat neatly on the stand.

Lexie slipped her feet into black heels with a delicate strap around her ankles before she leaned back in the chair. Her thoughts found Stephanie and the guilt of what she had put her best friend through over the past year. Stephanie was a rare treasure, a friend Lexie wanted to repay for all that she had done. Then there was Evan who walked the same line as she did, they were both fragments of the people they had once been. She wasn't sure how he would deal with her being taken.

Lexie looked down at the red material that hugged her curves so tightly she felt exposed. She ran her fingers over the swell of her breasts and flashes of Jackson's face pulled at her attention. The way he had ignited her body was hard to ignore but now with those memories came a rushing anger. She tightened her hands into fists and took a deep breath. She had unfinished business with Jackson and she wished more than anything she would be able to deliver the message. She knew if she held on to this anger she would be able to accomplish what she needed. Anger unlike pain made her feel invincible when it burned hot.

Lexie stood up when someone unlocked her door. She forced her hands to relax, and gave her body a quick shake to loosen herself up so she didn't appear tense. She was surprised to see John enter the room. A smile pulled at his features unnaturally as he laid eyes upon her.

"Lexie, glad to see you're ready," John said casually. If he was surprised he gave no hint of it in his voice.

"Yes, well, I'm actually looking forward to leaving this room." Lexie forced a smile. She tried to make her posture seem relaxed despite the turmoil in her stomach.

"You look just like your mother," John said with what appeared to be a flash of emotion but it was gone as quick as it came. She was again left looking at the soulless man before her. She tried not to study his features too much for fear that she would recognize herself.

John swung the door open. "Come." Unlike Flint, John did not offer his arm as he led the way. Two of John's men followed closely behind her, allowing her little space to distance herself from John.

As soon as they stepped off the elevator, Lexie could hear the music and the stream of voices floating down the hall. John led her toward the banquet room she had been taken to on her first day. Men mingled around the room in a mixture of attire. A bar was set up on one end and a band was playing in the corner. The music was a very soothing melody that blended in the background. The female singer's voice was gritty and powerful as it hummed through the room. She was an unusual beauty with wideset eyes and hair that was the color of strawberries. She was captivating as she sang to the crowd.

Lexie looked at the men around the room. Some looked as if they'd just walked off the street while others wore suits that spoke of money. It was strange to see the unusual mix of people all together in one place.

A waiter approached John as soon as he walked in the room, offering a glass of red wine on his tray. John accepted the glass and was immediately swept up in conversations from a few suits eager for his attention.

"You look lovely." Lexie spun around to see

Flint standing behind her. Her heart exploded in a frenzied pace. It was time to step into the ring.

"Thank you." She offered him a tentative smile. "What is the cause for celebration? Is it the annual bank robbers' gala?" Lexie tried to keep her breathing calm.

Flint chuckled and held out a glass of wine for her. "For some that would actually be quite fitting."

Lexie accepted, making sure to brush against his hand with hers. "Are you my watch dog for the evening?" Lexie allowed a teasing tone to caress her words and she could see Flint take the bait when his eyes turned dark.

"You could say that."

"Am I to keep my mouth shut and just sip on wine?" She tipped the glass to her lips and looked up at him.

"That would be wise." Flint raised his brow.

Lexie took a sip of the sweet wine and tried to ignore the stares from the questionable characters. She counted twenty-nine men with the exception of John's muscle that were stationed around the exterior of the room. She felt naked under the sea of eyes, reminding her of how Flint made her feel in the hotel room. She swallowed the lump in her throat, trying to conjure up the girl she met in the mirror. It was her time to shine.

Lexie listened to the singer and kept to herself as Flint was drawn into conversation by a group of men that looked like bankers, with brown suits and thick rimmed glasses. They seemed to be reserved when it came to details as they spoke, indicating that their business was not legitimate. Lexie tried not to think about what all these men in the room were capable of if they were involved with John Stodden. They must know what type of man he was…she wondered what that made them.

Lexie noticed a group of women enter the room. She recognized a few from earlier that day when Miller had returned her to her room. They filed in with lazy, seductive smiles upon their faces. They looked like they were under the influence of something, the way they stared blankly around the room. The serious mood of the room changed dramatically as the men were given a new focus.

Lexie watched the girls mingle with the men as she stayed tucked away near the side of the room. Flint kept throwing her glances as he continued speaking to the "Bankers," a conversation that quickly became heated. Lexie tried to pick up on any details she could, but they kept their voices low as she lingered on the outside of their circle. They apparently did not fall for the scantily-clad distractions wandering around the room as they barely even glanced at the women vying for attention. They stayed focused on dealing with their issues despite the atmosphere.

Lexie was relieved when Flint passed her off on Miller and led the group of men out of the room. Miller had been standing on the sidelines and gave her a genuine smile as she leaned against the wall next to him. "Interesting party." Lexie smiled.

"Yeah, I'm kind of surprised John let you come. These things tend to get…" Miller trailed off as if trying to find the right word.

"X-rated?" Lexie had a feeling she knew where

things were leading. There was too much promise of sex in the eyes of the women hanging off the arms of the men not to deliver.

"Yeah," Miller smiled uncomfortably. "My name is Chad, by the way, but most people call me Miller."

"Lexie." She smiled and sipped on her wine. "I'm starting to think that John allowing me to come was another one of his scare tactics." Lexie knew exactly what this was. It was another way for John to let her know he was in control. He wanted her to see this and know that if she didn't follow his rules that she could be one of the girls, high as a kite and wandering around offering themselves. She wondered why these women would ever agree to this.

"About earlier…" Miller started.

"Thank you for that," Lexie said, cutting him off, placing her hand on his shoulder. "It meant a lot to hear her voice."

Miller nodded his head and scanned the room. "I can't do it again."

"I know," Lexie said, letting her hand fall away. She tipped her glass up, draining the rest of her wine.

Lexie let her eyes wander around the room and wondered if any of these men had families at home as they allowed their sexual instincts to take front and center stage. The scene continued to unfold in front of her as she began her second glass of wine. Flint hadn't returned and John was nowhere to be seen. She wondered if she had been forgotten as the evening progressed and other matters tied up John and Flint.

Lexie flattened her back against the wall when two men approached her, their eyes like a starving animal as they took her in. Lexie folded her arms and squared her jaw. She would offer nothing to these men, not even a polite smile. Miller stepped in front of her, blocking her view of the men. "She's off limits. Move along." The two men sauntered away, throwing hungry looks over their shoulder s until another woman grabbed their attention. Lexie breathed a sigh of relief as she relaxed against the wall.

"I think maybe I should take you back to your room," Miller said, turning around to meet her troubled expression. Most of the women who had entered with flashy dresses were now completely nude except for their impossible heels. They were openly fondled by the men in their company without discretion.

Lexie watched the brunette with the leopard print shoes unbuckle the pants of one of the men in a suit. He stared down at her intensely as he drained his glass. She leaned over, seductively licking her lips as she pulled him free of his pants and stroked him before she took him in her mouth. She looked up at him and batted her eyes to expertly draw on his pleasure. Another man standing nearby unfastened his pants. He approached the brunette from behind. He ran his fingers along her opening before he slid himself into her. He thrust hard and fast and made her gag around the other man still in her mouth.

Lexie's mouth fell open in shock. The room quickly unravelled and smell of sex permeated her senses. If she hadn't seen it with her own eyes she wouldn't have believed it. A woman's scream tore through the music in the room. Lexie stood on her toes to see the nervous looking girl she had seen earlier in the hallway. There was a panicked look on her face as a man ripped her dress open. She was surrounded by a few others, all looking on hungrily.

Lexie stepped toward her but Miller grabbed her shoulder. "I need to get you out of here."

"But the girl..." Lexie spun around in horror.

"She signed up for it. We can't help her," Miller said sternly. "Let's go."

"We can't just leave her." Lexie pushed his arm away but Miller grabbed her hand.

"Yes, we can." Miller pulled her toward the door. "My orders were to make sure you weren't touched." Lexie's eyes filled with unshed tears. She desperately wanted to help the girl. Those animals would eat her alive because they were not men, they were monsters. Lexie yanked her arm free of Miller's hold but he grabbed her shoulder and pushed her from the room.

"How can you stand this?" Lexie questioned in disbelief.

"Be quiet, Lexie. You're gonna get us both in trouble." Miller led her toward the elevator doors. "I'm just as stuck here as you are. There's nothing I can do, either."

Lexie looked up into his eyes and realized the truth. He was just as much of a prisoner as she was.

Lexie walked numbly toward the elevator following Miller. When the doors opened she stepped on, anxious to get as far from it as she could. There was a man standing in the elevator who gave her a quick once over before turning his attention back to his phone. He looked to be a polished man and his suit definitely looked expensive, but all thoughts faded away when she noticed the scar on his neck. Her mother's warning hung heavy in her mind as she pressed herself against the opposite side of the elevator. Miller noticed her discomfort and stood between them, blocking her view.

As soon as the elevator doors opened, Lexie dashed out. Miller grabbed for her but her arms slipped through his hold. "Lexie!" Miller called out after her. As soon as she rounded the corner, she slowed her pace to let Miller catch up with her.

"Do you know who that man was on the elevator?" Lexie asked as she continued slowly up the hallway. Miller looked relieved he didn't have to chase her.

"Yeah, he's Mayor Terence Masten of Belhaven." Miller looked back over his shoulder to confirm they were alone.

"He's a mayor?" Lexie gasped, keeping her voice low.

"Yeah."

"Does he have anything to do with John?"

"Yes, he comes here every once in a while to see John behind closed doors."

"Miller." They both turned when Flint called to Miller from down the hall. Lexie turned around to see him heading in their direction. Flint's tie was loosened he looked as though he had been drinking. "You're needed downstairs. I'll see Lexie to her room."

Miller nodded before heading back down the hall. Lexie took a deep breath and kept walking toward room 324, her prison.

Flint didn't say anything as he matched her pace and then opened her door when they stopped in front of it. Lexie brushed past him. She closed her eyes tight, hoping he would lock the door behind her and leave. Instead, he followed her inside.

CHAPTER TEN

John

John looked at his own reflection in the surface of the mirrored coffee table before he focused his attention on the lines of cocaine that obstructed his view. He picked up a straw and inhaled the bitter powder. The rush was immediate and satisfying as it hit the back of his throat.

He looked around the room with new eyes as he picked up his glass of whiskey and leaned back on the sofa. His new business partner, Brian Crothers, sat to his right, a smudge of white dust under his nose as he drank in the entertainment that had drawn much of the business conversations to a minimum. The man loved his blow as well as many of the other luxuries in life but he was a solid partner. Their plans to open Bitter Sweet were going ahead flawlessly. The private gentleman's club offering exclusive memberships already had a waitlist as they approached the grand opening. Four other men sat around the room, all involved to some degree in the new business endeavor, but currently seemed unable to form any type of coherent thought.

Rebecca sat to his left wearing a formal dress he had purchased for her to satisfy her tastes for finery. She always looked the part with her sinful curves and full lips but John could no longer stand looking at her. She only reminded him of everything she wasn't. She ran her hand up and down his thigh, trying to elicit a response from him, but he pushed her hand away. It did not seem to deter her, as she remained persistent.

Two women were the centerpiece of activity in the room. A naked blonde was bent over the arm of the sofa. Her hands splayed in front of her as her heavy breasts swayed with her movements. She appeared to be lost in the throes of the natural rhythm of her pleasure as she rocked her hips but John didn't miss her quick glances toward the mountain of blow on the table. He knew that look in her eye. She was an addict and she did whatever she could to find her next hit. She was a pretty girl without tattoos or any outward signs of an unfortunate life. This girl wore her scars deep, the best kind for this line of work. He knew her type well.

A curvy brunette dressed in only a strap-on slid her fingers deep inside the blonde, thrusting them in and out as she licked the sensitized flesh. Soon the blonde's excitement was dripping freely from her center. The brunette withdrew her fingers and seductively slid them into her mouth as she looked John in the eye. John appreciated her eagerness to please as he stared back at her. He could see the desperation hidden in her eyes and he found it more desirable than the show she was providing. This girl wanted power and she knew exactly who held it.

She grabbed the blonde's hips and positioned the dildo at her entrance before plunging it deep inside her until their skin slapped together. Their breasts bounced from the vigorous movements as the brunette continued to plunge inside her repeatedly. The blonde cried out in a strangled moan and it plucked John's desire. The erotic display of watching a woman take another made his sexual need pull at his groin. Thoughts of Mary began to filter into his mind and his erection flared to life, demanding a taste of what he truly wanted.

The door opened and Rayner walked into the room. "I have the update you were looking for, Boss," Rayner said, crossing his arms, his attention not wavering to the erotic display taking place mere feet from him.

"Let's have it then." John looked up at Rayner.

"Lexie was returned to her room. She looked a little shaken," Rayner informed him.

"Good." John ran his fingers through his hair.

"And Aiello called to say that the meeting is all set up and Jackson and his men should be arriving shortly," Rayner continued.

"Make sure Aiello knows that none of them are to leave alive. Where's Flint?" John leaned forward and grabbed the bottle of whiskey off the table and refilled his glass.

"With Lexie." Rayner gave his head a slight tilt but it was enough of an indication to let John know that he wasn't sure what Flint was up to.

"Is that so? Make sure things stay in hand with our other guests," John ordered.

"Yes, sir." Rayner gave him a nod before taking his leave.

John leaned back and ran his hand down his tie. He had noticed Flint's fascination with Lexie. He realized now that he might have to set some boundaries for him when it came to her.

Brian was on the edge of his seat, practically salivating as he watched the women. The brunette continued to penetrate the blonde as she fondled her breasts. She squeezed and pulled her nipples as she quickened her pace. The blonde's body was tensing as her pleasure built.

"Feel free to test the merchandise." John waved his hand toward the women.

Brian's eyes lit up as he set his glass down on the table and stood up. He grabbed for his belt as he walked up behind the brunette. John drained his glass and discarded it on the table.

He stood up and buttoned his jacket.

"Where are you going?" Rebecca grabbed for his hand but he pulled it away.

"The time for business has passed. Enjoy the evening, gentlemen," John addressed everyone in the room.

"You're not leaving me here." Rebecca grabbed his jacket. John hit her across the face with the back of his hand.

"Don't touch me, bitch." John straightened his jacket and looked down at her tear-filled eyes as she held her cheek. "I think you need a reminder of your place."

John turned around and pointed toward two men on the other side of the room. "Show Rebecca what whores are good for."

"No…John," Rebecca pleaded. John stepped out of her reach. He could see the fear in her eyes. If she was under the belief that he cared for her she was stupider than he originally thought. She was as disposable as any of the women he brought in.

John walked out into the hallway to the destination that called to him on a primal level. He stopped in front of the unnumbered door and took pause. He thrived on knowing what he wanted was in his grasp, but now the wait was over. He wanted a taste and he wanted it now. He had been denied long enough.

John pulled the key from his pocket and opened the door. "Hello, Mary," John's words were heavy with intention as he walked into the room. He could hear her whimper before he swung the door shut behind him.

CHAPTER ELEVEN

Jackson

Jackson pulled the car into the parking lot of Bella Italia and cut the engine. The building, although fairly new, had an old world charm to it with rustic beams and stonework on the front of the building.

"Am I the only one who has a bad feeling about this?" Dane asked, looking around the parking lot suspiciously.

"No. I've had a bad feeling ever since I laid eyes on Jackson," Evan complained.

"Fuck you, Evan," Jackson said with a shake of his head.

"How do we know what this Steven guy looks like?" Dane asked as he leaned between the seats.

"No clue, but I'm sure we'll see him lurking around," Jackson said as he checked the time.

"Do you think we can actually order some food? I'm fucking starving," Teddy said, rubbing his stomach.

101

"Let's just hope we don't get shot," Jackson replied with a raised brow.

"Too late," Dane added, patting his side. "I already covered that part."

"Evan, you stay in the car." Jackson turned around in his seat to lay eyes on him.

"Yeah, whatever. I've had enough excitement for one day anyway."

"Text us if anything looks suspicious," Teddy ordered him.

"Leave the keys so I can at least listen to some music." Evan held out his hand.

"Nope." Jackson opened his door and stepped out onto the pavement. He could hear Evan complaining but he ignored him.

Jackson wasn't used to the restricted feeling of a suit. He straightened his tie and gave his shoulders a shake to loosen himself up. He couldn't even remember the last time he had worn one.

"Man, I look fucking amazing in this suit," Teddy said, walking around the front of the car as he rubbed his hands down the front of his jacket. "We need a picture of this." Teddy spun around and held up his phone to take a picture of all three of them. "Say cheese, bitches."

Jackson gave him the middle finger impatiently as he searched the nearby cars for any sign of someone who could be their guy. They had ten minutes until they had to be through the front doors.

"Oh come on, Jacks, this was for our kids one day." Teddy sulked as he looked at the picture.

"Like anyone would have kids with you," Jackson retorted.

"Accidents do happen." Teddy winked.

"Let's hope they don't for the sake of the world." Dane stretched his tall frame, careful not to irritate his side. He pulled out a bottle of pills from his pocket, popped the top, and tipped it to his lips.

"I think that's our man." Jackson pointed toward a gentleman who climbed out of a silver Honda Civic. He wore a brown wool suit and a red plaid tie that resembled a Halloween costume more than evening attire.

"Where the fuck did this guy come from?" Teddy asked in disbelief.

"Max dug him up from some shithole, I'm sure." Jackson rubbed forehead in annoyance.

"Jackson?" the man asked as he approached, looking nervous.

"Yeah," Jackson responded bluntly.

Steven looked skittish as stopped in front of Jackson. "Aiello has requested we keep our mouths shut and do not speak until we are directed to the meeting area. He will not tolerate any disturbances in his restaurant and guns are prohibited."

"Fuck no. I'm not walking in there unarmed," Dane declared.

"We don't have a choice, Dane," Jackson said determinedly. "What other options do we have to get our hands on the hardware we need?"

"I think I was high when I agreed to this." Dane rubbed his hand down his face.

"You're always fucking high," Teddy said with a laugh.

Jackson opened the trunk and placed his guns inside. Dane and Teddy followed suit before they followed Steven toward the front entrance of the restaurant. Delicious smells met them when they pulled opened the doors. The interior was dimly lit with a large stone fireplace in the center of the dining room. White clothed tables were placed throughout the space with strategically placed dividers to give guests the illusion of privacy.

The hostess greeted them with a smile that broadened as they approached. She ignored Steven as she addressed Jackson, Dane, and Teddy, who towered over his short stature. Steven cleared his throat to capture her attention. "Good evening, do you have a reservation?" she asked. Jackson was surprised Teddy didn't jump in with the invitation. He was always one to take advantage of a woman's attention, especially an attractive one like the petite blonde waiting on them.

Steven handed her a card. She glanced at it and her smile fell away. "Follow me." She led them toward the back of the restaurant to a private room. "I'll let Mr. Aiello know you're here." She closed the door behind them, leaving them alone.

"At least it's nice," Dane said, looking around at the décor. The walls were deep red, and an ornate chandelier hung over a large rectangular table that looked like it was cut from an old slab of wood. It spanned the length of the room and sat eighteen people. "How wrong can this meeting go inside his restaurant with all those people out there? He wouldn't cause a scene in a place like this," Dane suggested, seemingly trying to convince himself that he would be all right without his guns.

Steven fidgeted with his ancient looking suit and

snapped his gum repeatedly in his mouth. He avoided eye contact with any of them.

"How do you know Max?" Jackson asked curiously.

Steven glanced up at him before he frowned. "Our paths crossed years ago. He saved my ass so I owe him," Steven said, shuffling his feet.

"Let me guess...someone wanted to kill you," Dane suggested.

Steven scratched at his neck, making his skin turn a bright shade of red. He pulled at his tie, loosening it. "Yeah," he finally admitted. "That pretty much covers it."

"If you keep snapping that gum I'm gonna feel like killing you," Jackson said irritably.

Steven's eyes widened to saucers before he swallowed his gum in an exaggerated gulp.

The door opened and a raven-haired waitress came in carrying a tray of wine glasses and a bottle of wine. "Good evening, gentlemen. Mr. Aiello should be with you shortly, but he sent in this bottle of wine to thank you for your patience." Her deep red lips curled up into a flirtatious smile when her gaze fell on Jackson. "It's our best and sure to please your palate."

Jackson looked at Teddy with a scowl. Something was definitely off. There was no way if he was in his right mind that he would leave that comment alone. Teddy had a faraway look in his eyes as he watched the girl pour the wine. He threw Dane a curious glance, but he only shrugged his shoulders, not knowing why Teddy was acting strange either.

"You all right, man?" Jackson asked Teddy.

"Yeah, don't worry about me. I'm on," Teddy dismissed quickly. Jackson wasn't convinced but they didn't have time to deal with any personal issues right now. They all knew there were some things left buried but this seemed different. Something was on Teddy's mind and it had been since they left Max's rundown apartment building. Ever since he retrieved that camera from that woman's room he had seemed a bit distracted.

"Thanks, Sweetheart." Dane accepted the glass of wine she offered him. After she handed everyone a full glass, she set the bottle on the table and left the room. Jackson smelled the full-bodied wine before setting the glass down on the table. He needed perfect clarity for this plan to work. Dane and Teddy followed suit. They were always ones to stay focused on the goal at hand. Steven, on the other hand, guzzled his entire glass and wiped his face with the back of his hand before eyeing their untouched glasses. "Are you gonna drink those?"

"Help yourself." Jackson waved toward their wine.

"Fuck, man. Let me guess, you're an alcoholic too?" Dane asked, taking a seat. His face showed his relief as he sat down, favoring his side. Jackson knew Dane would keep going no matter how much pain he was in. It was a quality that made him exceptional at what he did. He never let anything get in his way.

Steven ignored him as he grabbed for another glass. Jackson pulled his phone from his pocket to make sure Evan didn't message him. They were all getting restless as they waited for the meeting to begin.

Jackson dropped down in one of the chairs and kicked Teddy's leg. "What's up, man? You have been fucking daydreaming since Max's apartment. What happened with that girl?"

Teddy looked up at Jackson as he bit his lip thoughtfully. "Nothing happened. I don't know, but there's something about her I can't seem to shake."

"What girl are you talking about?" Dane's attention was piqued.

The door opened and all of them turned to see a large man walk in the door. His salt and pepper hair was slicked back. He wore a black suit with a white shirt that stretched across his round stomach. He was closely followed by four men all dressed similarly as they filed in behind him.

Jackson and the others stood as they rounded the table. "Steven," the large man greeted curtly.

Steven nodded uncomfortably. "Mr. Aiello."

Aiello's breathing was exceptionally labored, a sign that his size was a strain on his body. "I see that you drank your wine. I hope it was to your satisfaction." He sat down on the opposite side of the table with a groan.

"It was," Jackson confirmed politely.

"It is one of my favorites from my home country." Aiello reached for the empty bottle sitting on the table. "You see it has a rich, full-bodied flavor like a punch to the palate." He brought the bottle to his nose and inhaled deeply. "Did you pick up on the wild berry and spices?"

"It was great. Thank you for your hospitality, but

we are short on time." Jackson tried to be polite about rushing the conversation ahead. "We would like to jump right to business if we can."

Aiello sat the bottle down on the table. "Yes, yes. Let's get to business, shall we. Steven informed me you are in need of guns." Aiello flattened his hands upon the table as his eyes traveled over them. Steven made a strange, garbled noise in response. Everyone looked to see him suddenly clawing at his throat, trying to draw breath.

"What the fuck?" Jackson stood up. He glanced at Aiello, who had a satisfied smile on his face. Jackson knew immediately that he was not surprised that Steven was suddenly suffocating. Jackson grabbed his empty glass and smelled the contents.

"You won't detect the poison. That is the beauty of the wine. It masks the flavor." Aiello leaned back in his chair. "After I spoke with Steven, I received a call from none other than John Stodden."

Jackson dropped the glass and it shattered on top of the table, sending shards scattering in all directions. "Apparently he wants you dead and he was willing to make it worth my while." Jackson knew they were in trouble. The men with Aiello were all armed and they were at a huge disadvantage.

"You motherfuck—"Jackson grabbed for his throat, pulling at his tie. He gasped loudly as he pulled his tie loose. Dane and Teddy caught on and followed suit.

"I'm sure you can understand that he made an offer I couldn't refuse. It's just business, after all."

Aiello's deep laugh rumbled through the room.

Jackson grabbed the edge of the table, leaning over and gasping. When Aiello turned around to address his men, Jackson made his move. He grabbed the edge of the table and threw his weight into it as he lifted it and flipped the large table on top of Aiello before his men had time to react. Aiello screamed out as the weight of the table crashed down on him and sent him to the ground.

Teddy and Jackson both lunged over the table at the men scrambling for their weapons. They took them down and struggled to gain the upper hand. Jackson grabbed the gun of the man who had succeeded in pulling it from his holster. He forced the gun up under his chin and pulled the trigger. Blood sprayed over the faces of the others as they lunged toward Jackson. Jackson turned the gun on them and they were dead before they hit the ground. Teddy had his hands around the last one's throat and squeezing as the man tried to reach for his gun on the floor.

Dane kicked it out of the man's hand when he wrapped his fingers around it and stomped down on the man's face, snapping his neck. "I had him," Teddy gasped as he pushed himself off the man whose face was now caved in.

"I'm just trying to speed this show up because the entire restaurant heard those gunshots. It's fucking chaos out there," Dane said. He grabbed Teddy's hand and pulled him to his feet.

"Jacks, you all right?" Teddy asked as they both turned toward Jackson.

"I will be in a minute," Jackson said as he

walked over to Aiello, pinned under the table. The man couldn't manage any words as the weight of the table crushed his chest. His breath was now desperate as he fought to pull air into his lungs.

"I'm sure you can understand. It's just business," Jackson said, stepping on Aiello's throat, slowly forcing his weight down until his eyes bulged from his head and the light faded from his eyes.

Jackson stared down at Aiello's red eyes that stared back at him lifelessly. "We have to go, Jacks," Teddy said as he tucked a pistol down the back of his pants. "The police will show up any minute."

"Yeah." Jackson grabbed a gun off the floor. Dane was already on the lookout at the door. "Everyone is making a run for it. Let's head toward the back." Dane slipped out the door.

Jackson followed close behind Dane as he headed toward the kitchen doors. A woman huddled behind the counter just inside the kitchen screamed when she saw Dane walk in.

"Whoa, sweetheart. We're just trying to get out of here." Dane raised his hands. "Shit's going sideways."

The terrified girl pointed toward the back corner of the kitchen just as three men came barreling through the door with guns. The men stopped short when they noticed them heading in their direction. Jackson, Dane, and Teddy dropped down behind a large island in the center of the kitchen while grabbing for their guns. Jackson peeked over the counter to get a visual on the men and someone shot toward him, barely missing. The bullet lodged in the cabinet behind him. Dane made his move and leaned around the island, shooting off three rounds.

"There's still one more. I can't fucking see him," Dane said, ducking back behind the island.

The girl was still huddled on the other side of the kitchen. She was completely frozen with fear and standing in a puddle of her own urine. Jackson watched her eyes as she looked across the kitchen. She told him exactly what he needed to know. Jackson stood up and shot the last man who was approaching around the island. The bullet caught him in the cheek and exploded through the other side of his face. He collapsed, taking out a stack of pots on his way down as he smeared blood all over the counter.

The girl started to scream again and made a run for the door leading toward the restaurant. Jackson headed toward the exit, jumping over the bodies of the men. Shoving open the steel door, Dane and Teddy filed out behind him into the back alley of the restaurant with their guns readied.

"I think we're clear. Let's get to the car and get the fuck out of here," Jackson said, tucking his gun under his arm so it was concealed from anyone who might see them. The people from the restaurant were all panicked as they filled the parking lot. There was no way they were getting their car through the mass of people running for their vehicles.

Evan was standing outside the car when they approached. "What the fuck happened in there?" he asked anxiously, his eyes flashing back and forth from Jackson to the people still funnelling out of the restaurant.

"A fucking shit storm. Grab your things. We're walking from here," Jackson said. He opened the door and grabbed a few items out of the glove box. He rounded the car and opened the trunk. Once they had everything they needed, they weaved through the cars and headed toward the street.

As soon as Jackson stepped foot onto the sidewalk, the police cars barrelled down the street with their sirens masking the hum of panicked voices.

"Keep walking." Jackson grabbed the back of Evan's shirt when he stopped to watch the scene unfold. Jackson needed to make sure the police didn't catch sight of them. No one spoke until they were blocks away and the sirens became a distant sound.

"Where are we walking to? Our hotel is fucking miles from here. How are we getting back?" Evan asked finally breaking the silence.

"Calm down, baby bro. Jackson always has a plan B."

A car pulled up beside them and drove up onto the sidewalk, barely missing them. "Whoa, what the fuck!" Teddy backed up.

Jackson cursed angrily when he recognized the driver.

"What's going on, Jacks?" Dane asked, his hand on the handle of his gun.

"This is our shitty plan B," Jackson said, spitting on the ground as the car door opened.

CHAPTER TWELVE

Stephanie

Stephanie leaned against the bars. They dug into her back but she didn't care, she was growing used to the discomfort of being locked in the small cell. She could no longer smell the damp putrid odor that lingered in the air of this place. It used to make her feel sick, but not anymore. She was acclimatizing to this shade of a life because her mind was beginning to betray her and believe this was her new home.

Stephanie tapped her fingers against her ribs. She couldn't escape the hard, uncomfortable ball of pain which had settled deep in her chest. It felt like she was going to choke on it if it grew any more.

Stephanie tried to envision who the girl was that had left the ring. She wondered if this poor woman was stuck within these walls for eternity, doomed to remain in this prison without any alleviation from the pain she had suffered. She hadn't believed in ghosts until now, but the feel of this place made her question everything. The air felt too thick, the darkness seemed filled with something when there should be nothing. She questioned if she was destined to the same fate. No tears came with these thoughts because she felt too numb. She had been avoiding sleep to stay awake as long as possible so when she finally did submit, it would be dreamless.

Her arms and legs ached uncomfortably from exhaustion and hunger burned a hole in her stomach as she sat on the cold, unyielding floor. She had counted every bar that caged her in and every crack in the floor. She felt like she knew this place better than the apartment she had lived in for the past two years.

Stephanie scrambled to her feet when she heard that disheartening sound of footsteps as they descended down the creaky steps. She held her breath and closed her eyes as she heard the door lock unlatch. She didn't want to see him enter; she didn't want to see him at all.

"Rose," he said in a pleased tone. "I have a surprise for you." He had called her Rose since she had first woken in this dungeon. She hadn't given it much thought, but now she wondered if Rose was the owner of the ring.

Stephanie crossed her arms and instinctively took a step backwards as he approached the bars. "Open your eyes, Rose." His voice made her shiver. Stephanie squeezed them tighter and shook her head. "Open them!" he hollered abruptly.

Stephanie snapped her eyes open. He grabbed the bars, rubbing his hands slowly down the smooth metal. The look in his eyes always terrified her, especially when he insisted on staring at her like he wanted to cut her open and see what was inside. A cold, sadistic smile spread across his face. "That's better. I brought you a treat." He reached into his pocket and pulled out a chocolate bar.

"I don't like chocolate," Stephanie responded in a quiet voice.

"Yes, you do." He pulled the key to her cell out of his pocket and opened the door. Stephanie backed up until the cold metal frame of the cot touched the back of her legs. He pulled open the wrapper and exposed the chocolate. "This is your favorite." He broke a piece off and held it out toward her mouth. He stepped closer and touched the chocolate to her lips.

Stephanie opened her mouth and accepted it, not knowing what else to do. She was famished because he hadn't brought her any other food since the day before. She wasn't expecting the satisfying flavor as the soft texture melted on her tongue. It tasted wonderful to her starved body.

He moaned as he watched her eat the chocolate. "That's a good girl." He folded the package and placed it back in his pocket. "You can have the rest afterward."

"After what?" Stephanie shivered in fear.

He touched her neck and Stephanie pulled back with a gasp.

"Everything is almost perfect," he said, unfazed by her reaction. "If you don't cooperate, I'll have to drug you again."

Stephanie shook her head erratically. "Please no."

"Come with me." He held out his hand.

She looked down at it without moving. "Where are you taking me?"

He pointed to the far corner of the room toward the small run of cabinets. Stephanie took a deep, shaky breath before she placed her hand in his. She didn't want to, but the threat of drugging her again terrified her. She was defenseless in that state.

He led her out of the cell. It was the first time that she had walked out on her own. She had dreamt of this moment but it brought no relief because she was scared it might be more terrifying on the other side of the bars.

He stopped in front of the cabinets and turned to look her in the eyes. "Don't move, Rose."

Stephanie nodded, unable to bring herself to speak. He turned around and lifted a few boxes off something that was draped in a black tarp-like material. He grabbed the fabric and pulled it off to reveal a chair that looked similar to a dentist chair but it had restraints for the arms and legs. A whimper escaped her lips as she looked at it. Stephanie glanced toward the door that led to her freedom. She wondered if she made a run for it if she could make it before he caught up to her.

When he turned away, she decided she needed to try. She thought it might be her only chance for escape. Blood rushed in her ears as she darted across the cold floor. The only thing she could see was the metal door on the other side of the room. Everything else blurred as she tried to keep her balance. The floor felt like it was moving under her feet as she fought light-headedness. Her fingers barely brushed the handle before she was shoved into the door by a crushing weight. Her head hit the door hard enough to disorient her. She could feel his breath on her neck as she attempted to struggle against his hold.

A sharp prick on her arm made her cry out ad she immediately began to feel the effects. Her arms and legs began to feel too heavy to move. Her eyes closed and she lost herself into the strange dream-filled state the drugs always took her.

CHAPTER THIRTEEN

Lexie

Lexie backed into the room, refusing to turn her back to Flint. She was aware of the fact that she was locked in a room with a wild animal. She needed to gain the upper hand without Flint knowing or she would fall victim to whatever he had planned.

"That was quite the party. Are all John's parties like that?" Lexie started slowly so she could gain her confidence. She tried not to look at the pocket he had slid his phone into. She wanted to get her hands on it without him knowing, and to do this, she knew she would have to take things further than she dared let herself imagine. She just had to make sure he didn't become suspicious of her intentions.

Flint shrugged his shoulders "Most, yes." Flint looked like a starved animal would look if a piece of meat was waved in front of its face.

"I like that dress," Flint said as he moved closer to her.

Lexie backed up. "I thought it was me you

liked." She raised her brow playfully. It was taking everything she had to act the part and be convincing. She concentrated on the girl she had seen in the mirror. She had no choice if she wanted her life back. She would walk whatever path would lead her home. His eyes met hers questioningly before his brow relaxed. She could tell he was falling for her bait.

"I like you much, much more," he clarified as his eyes skimmed over her entire body.

"I have a confession to make…" Lexie trailed off. She walked away from him toward her night stand before spinning around, playing nervously with her lip. The distance between them made it easier for her to think.

"What?" He tensed as he watched her pull her bottom lip between her fingers.

"When I first saw you…" Lexie closed her eyes and thought of the first time she saw Jackson. "It was like I was suddenly granted a wish I hadn't even known I had longed for." Lexie looked up and met his eyes. "Does that make sense?"

"Yes, I know exactly what you mean," Flint said as approached. Lexie felt the edge of the bed against her leg as Flint placed his hand on her cheek. She forced herself to lean into his hand and she closed her eyes so she didn't have to look into his. She was terrified she would see exactly what he was.

"It gives me something good to focus on while being locked in my room all day."

"I want you to be mine." Flint leaned in and pressed his lips against hers. "All mine," he whispered against her mouth before he tilted her head back and closed his mouth over hers. Lexie ignored the voice screaming inside her head. Her heart raced so fast she could taste the coppery taste of her own blood as it rushed through her body. She raised her shaky hands and wrapped them around Flint's waist and submitted to the kiss. He explored her mouth with his tongue, trying to taint her with his dark lust. She ran her hands around his waist and toward his pocket as discreetly as she could.

Lexie thought of her mother locked in that room. She had no idea what John was doing to her. This was a small price to pay when she considered what was at stake. He pulled the zipper down on the back of her dress and Lexie gasped.

Flint pushed her back against the bed before she had a chance to get a grip on the phone and began to pull down the top of her dress, tearing at the fabric. "I want you naked. I want to see you now." Flint fumbled with the fabric.

"Whoa," Lexie gasped. "Let's go slow." Lexie tried to smile when he looked at her face but it was frozen and refused to express any hint of happiness. Panic held her close to the edge. She needed to be smart about this before things went too far but all she could think about was the sickening feeling of what he was going to do to her.

He pulled down the fabric of her dress so she was left only in her underwear. She tried to grab for it but he refused to let her stay clothed. "You will be mine," he said, staring down at her body. He didn't even notice her discomfort was written all over her face. He was past caring about anything but his own sexual desires.

Flint slid his jacket off his arms and tossed it beside her on the bed before he dropped to his knees. He ran his hands down the inside of her thighs and she tried to stop her legs from trembling. "Do you want me?" Lexie only nodded her head. "Say that you want me, Lexie."

"I want you," Lexie whispered. Flint smiled and looked down at her body, stopping between her legs. Lexie turned her head and looked at his jacket. A thrill of excitement penetrated her fear like a sharp knife as she noticed the pocket was within reach.

Lexie moaned when she felt him run his fingers over her sex, only a thin piece of material separating them. She tried to sound as convincing as she could. His eyes flicked up toward hers before he brought his lips down against the skin of her thigh. He licked her flesh.

"Yes…" Lexie gasped, grabbing the blanket of the bed. She glanced up to make sure he wasn't looking. She slid her hand over until her fingers felt the cool hard surface of his phone.

"That feels so good," she moaned. Once she had a hold on it, she slipped it out and brought it up as she pretended to grab her hair. His attention was between her legs and he didn't notice when she slipped the phone under her pillow. Once she tucked it away, she knew she had to move fast in case it rang and he discovered she took it.

"Flint," Lexie called down to him as he curled his fingers under the waistband of her underwear. "We can't do this yet." Lexie scrambled for a convincing plan. "We can't do this behind John's back. What if he gets angry? We should tell him first."

He stopped moving as her words hit him. He stopped undoing his belt and ran his hand through his hair in frustration. He sighed loudly and stared at her silently for a moment, seemingly lost in thought. "You're right," he finally submitted.

Lexie sat up and picked up his jacket, holding it out for him. She managed a smile because of the relief that flowed through her so potently. He slid his arm in the jacket and let her assist him in pulling it on. He adjusted his shirt before he leaned in and kissed her. "I'll tell John and then we'll continue where we left off."

"I hope so." Lexie smiled.

His confidence didn't show in his eyes, making Lexie wonder if he thought there might be a possibility that John would not allow this to happen. It was all the hope she needed. She never wanted there to be a next time.

"You should go before we get caught," Lexie said, rubbing her hands down his chest.

He nodded solemnly before he headed toward the door. The sound of the lock was the most beautiful thing to her ears. She scrambled for the phone, desperate to make a call before she was discovered. She didn't even leave time to pull on clothes. She grabbed the phone and ran into the bathroom, shoving the chair under the handle.

She pressed the bottom of the screen and wanted to cry in relief when she noticed it wasn't locked. She thought about calling the police, but she had no idea what to tell them. Her fingers shook so bad she had to attempt to dial Stephanie's number four times before she got it correct. She needed to know Stephanie was all right before she could think clearly.

Her phone rang and rang until it went to her answering machine. She hung up and tried Evan's number. She needed to hear a familiar voice.

It rang three times before Evan answered. "Hello?"

"Evan, oh my god. It's so good to hear your voice. Is Stephanie with you?" Tears flooded Lexie's eyes as she spoke.

"Lexie?" Evan gasped in the phone. The sound of shuffling erupted on the line, it sounded like a struggle.

"Evan? What's happening?" Lexie asked as she wiped her eyes.

"Lexie, where are you?" Jackson's voice hit her hard in the stomach. Her eyes flashed up to the mirror to see herself standing naked in the bathroom. She grabbed for the robe on the back of the door and frantically pulled it on.

"I don't know." So many emotions bubbled in her chest at the sound of his voice. "I stole this phone. I don't have long before they find out I have it. Is Stephanie with you too?"

"What are you talking about? She was taken with you and your mother," Jackson replied.

"What? No...she's not here. Oh my god, Jackson," Lexie gasped as she pulled on the ties of the robe until it dug into her waist.

"Calm down. We'll find her. Give me something so I can figure out where you are," Jackson said

123

determinedly.

Lexie wasn't sure if she could even trust Jackson, but if Evan was with him, it needed to count for something. She knew he was probably the best chance she had at getting out of here. She threw caution to the wind and decided to give him a chance. She would deal with the rest if she ever got out of here. "Um…I was blindfolded when they drove us here. I lost track of time." Lexie found it difficult to talk as she forced her words through her tight throat. "I know it was still dark when we got here. I think we're in some kind of hotel under construction. I'm in room 324. I don't know much else."

"I know where you are. I'm coming for you, Lex."

"Jackson…" Lexie began but couldn't finish.

"Did he hurt you?" Jackson cut in.

Lexie took a deep breath. "I'm fine, but I don't know about my mother. They won't let me see her." Lexie covered her mouth with her hand so Jackson couldn't hear her cry. She heard a sound in the hallway that made her panic.

"I have to go. I think someone is coming. I have to get rid of this phone."

"I'm coming for you."

Lexie hit end and dropped the phone on the floor. She grabbed the metal garbage bin. She knelt down and began hitting the phone, trying to break it in smaller pieces. When the phone finally submitted to her assault, she collected all the fragments and tossed them into the toilet a few at a time and flushed them away until there was no trace left.

Once it was gone, she blasted the hot water in the shower and climbed in. She wanted to wash off Flint's touch and calm her rattled nerves.

CHAPTER FOURTEEN

Jackson

Jackson looked down at Evan's phone. Lexie had sounded so terrified on the other end of the line. Every scenario within his scope of imagination plagued him and fueled his anger. The only thought that made the whole situation bearable was imagining how he would deliver the fatal blow to John Stodden when he killed him.

"Let me go." Evan struggled against Teddy's hold.

"You can let him go, Teddy," Jackson said, holding out Evan's phone. "I'm done."

Evan straightened his shirt and grabbed the phone from Jackson. "I wanted to talk to her," Evan didn't even try to contain his anger as he pulled up his screen looking for the number Lexie called from.

"You won't get her. She said she was going to get rid of the phone."

Evan glared at Jackson. "Why didn't you let me

talk to her?"

"I needed to find out where she was," Jackson answered without remorse. He just got confirmation of her location and now there was only one more thing standing in his way.

"And did you?" Evan asked, dropping his arm. He looked at the phone and saw Jackson was right. It was a private caller and didn't even yield a number in his call history.

"Yes." Evan's eyes widened as he looked at Jackson. "And we're going to get her once I deal with this little problem," Jackson said, pointing at the man leaning against the car.

"Hey now, Jacks. Is that how you refer to an old friend?" The man threw his cigarette down on the ground and placed his hand against his chest.

"You were never my fucking friend, Slash," Jacks replied emotionlessly.

"True," Slash admitted with a mock frown. "I still don't care much for you, to be honest."

"The feeling is mutual," Jackson retorted.

Slash had long scars that ran down the sides of his face and had a look in his eye that made people turn and walk the other way. He told people that he had gotten the scars in a bar fight but Jackson always suspected that they were self-inflicted. Slash had a fascination with cutting and pain. Most of his exposed skin had scars of various types that he wore like trophies. Unfortunately, his sick obsession also extended to cutting others. Jackson had been witness to his obsession first hand and Slash's talent with knives was the inspiration behind's Black's appreciation for the blade. They both liked the art of intimidation and knives were quite effective.

"What the fuck do you want? I don't have time for your games," Jackson said angrily when Slash pulled out another cigarette.

"Black wants to talk to you," Slash said. He took a deep pull from his cigarette and let the smoke escape the side of his mouth.

"Well, tell him to give me a call," Jackson bit off in irritation. He heard a vehicle pull up beside them and turned to see a black utility van. Someone rounded the vehicle and opened up the back doors.

"This is him calling," Slash said with a sadistic smile. "Get in the van." Slash pointed toward the opened rear.

"Why the fuck would I do that?" Jackson asked in disbelief.

"Do you see those men over there?" Slash tapped the ash off the end of his cigarette as he nodded his head toward a group of four men standing on the other side of the road. One of them waved back. "Their orders are to go into that coffee shop and shoot the place up if you all don't fucking get in the back of the van."

"Is he serious?" Evan burst out in alarm.

"Unfortunately, yes," Jackson said. He clenched his jaw and stared at Slash in utmost hatred. "I'll go." Jackson motioned toward his friends. "But Black has no business with them."

"I said *all* of you," Slash warned.

He waved his hand and the men across the street began walking toward the entrance of the coffee shop. "Okay, okay, you made your point. Call off your dogs," Jackson said with a shake of his head.

His patience was thin at best.

"And just when I thought things were starting to get boring," Teddy said lightly.

The man holding the doors open grabbed a small milk crate from the back. "Weapons in here." Jackson withdrew his guns and placed them inside before he climbed in the back of the van. The others followed after they too were disarmed. Jackson kicked a few dirty rags out of the way before he sat down on the floor of the van.

"Does the shit ever stop? How are we supposed to rescue the girls with all these psychos kidnapping us?" Evan blurted angrily at Jackson when the doors were closed behind them. A man who shut the back door climbed into the passenger's seat and told the driver to head out. He turned around in the seat, looking at the four of them sprawled out in the back.

"Don't try anything," he warned, holding his gun up to reinforce his threat.

"We wouldn't dream of it." Jackson said sarcastically.

"Feel free to swing this baby through a drive through. I could really use a cheeseburger right now," Teddy added. The men ignored him and turned up the music.

Dane tried to adjust himself comfortably against the side of the van but gave up with a sigh of frustration. He pulled up his shirt to peel back his bandage.

"That doesn't look good, man." Jackson raised his brow.

"Yeah well, when my doctor said bedrest, she

probably didn't mean partaking in any of the shit we're doin'." Dane laughed as he refastened the bandage.

"Yeah, sorry about the shitstorm," Jackson said.

"Dane wouldn't know what to do with himself if his life wasn't being threatened. He'd go fucking crazy," Teddy said, kicking Dane's foot.

"What's life without blood and pain?" Dane said as he gently patted his side.

"You are all shades of fucked up," Evan said, shaking his head. "You're all fucking cops who I've only seen acting like criminals. How do guys like you even get badges?"

"Even the good guys need someone to clean up the shit," Teddy said, giving Evan an affectionate rub on the top of his head. Evan pulled away with a dirty look.

"Lexie said Stephanie isn't with them," Jackson said, breaking the mood. "She didn't even know she was taken."

"What?" Evan blurted. "Where the fuck is she, then?"

"He must be keeping her separate," Teddy suggested.

"At least we know where to look," Jackson confirmed. "If she's there, we'll find her."

Evan raked his hands through his hair. "What good does it fucking do if we're now being held by one of your old boyfriends?"

"I think this will actually work to our benefit," Jackson said, feeling good about the potential opportunity Black's involvement might bring.

"How so?"

***

The rear doors to the van swung open to reveal the interior of a parking garage. The man from the passenger's seat stood back as he motioned for them to get out with a wave of his gun. Jackson helped Dane to his feet and jumped out of the back.

They were led through a set of doors and down various hallways until music began filtering through the walls. A few shady looking characters lingered in the hall smoking pot. One of them with a leather vest and bald head blew smoke in Jackson's face. He sneered and revealed he was missing a few of his teeth. Jackson ignored him.

Slash stopped in front of a door that pulsed from the base of the music blaring on the other side. He and the other men tucked away their guns. "Don't try anything stupid," Slash warned.

Jackson raised his hands. "Never do."

He could hear Dane snicker behind him.

"Through here." Slash opened the door. Heavy music poured out to meet them from what appeared to be a nightclub. It wasn't long before he realized what type of place this was. Women danced on various stages throughout the main bar area. Countless men and the odd woman filled the bar to capacity, eager to watch the provocative entertainment. The women on stage did not disappoint. They knew how to win the crowd as they kept their audience wanting more.

They continued past what was the largest of the stages, filled with multiple poles that were all being utilized, and toward a back room.

Jackson glanced behind him to notice on of Black's men nudging Evan to keep moving. Evan looked a little awestruck by the naked women. Jackson followed Slash and the others as they walked into a hallway lined with multiple doors. A woman was standing halfway down the hall dressed in only a thong as she argued on her cellphone.

"Take it somewhere else, Mindy," Slash called to her. She spun around and narrowed her eyes before stomping off and disappearing into one of the rooms.

Slash knocked on an unmarked door before he partially opened it wide enough to step inside. "I have Jackson and his men," he announced.

"Send Jackson in." Black instructed. It seemed like a different life when he had been a part of Black's crew so many years ago. It was a time that he had planned to never return to, but life had a way of throwing you into the very thing you wanted to avoid.

Slash opened the door for Jackson but stopped the others from following. "Just Jackson." He slipped out of the room and shut the door.

"Jackson Finley, it's been a long time." Black sat back in his desk chair. The last ten years had aged him considerably. His black hair was now mostly white and he now wore a full beard. It took Jackson a moment to recognize the man he once knew. His office was decorated minimally compared to the tacky décor outside the office. A few framed photographs hung on the wall. A small bar sat in the corner and there was a sitting area next to it with a couple of black sofas.

"Yeah, a few years," Jackson said conservatively. He knew Black did not favor his unceremonious departure. No one was allowed to leave Black's company without his approval but Jackson did just that.

"It doesn't look like running off to become a cop saved your soul. You're back crawling in the trenches with the rest of us." Black closed his laptop in front of him and waved to the seat in front of his desk.

"I'm a sucker for punishment, I guess," Jackson said as he dropped into the club chair.

"It seems so." Black pulled open his desk drawer and picked up a Ruger handgun and placed it on the desk in front of him.

Jackson looked down at the gun and frowned. "I thought you were a blade guy."

"Depends on my mood." Black took a deep breath and looked at Jackson. "I was being paid a small fortune to keep Seth alive. He had family in powerful places."

"I was wondering why you didn't kill him when you found out he was skimming your product," Jackson said, the pieces finally coming into place. "How'd they feel about you removing some of his fingers?"

"I couldn't let him go completely unpunished now, could I?"

Jackson narrowed his eyes and leaned back in his seat. "So tell me why you haven't already put a bullet between my eyes."

"It has been brought to my attention recently that I am not the only one who wants you dead." Back raised his brow.

Jackson scratched his forehead thoughtfully. "It also seems like me and you have a common enemy," he said, watching Black's response. Jackson knew that Black would be able to see the bigger picture. Unlike Seth, who was always impulsive, Black had a mind for business and never let his emotions get in the way of opportunity.

"Tell me why John Stodden wants you dead so bad," Black inquired.

"He wants to eliminate a threat."

"And are you a threat to Stodden?" Black narrowed his eyes.

"If you consider the fact that I plan to kill him, then yes."

Black laughed and adjusted his weight in his chair. "What the fuck makes you think that you can even get close to him, let alone kill him?"

"If you don't think that I can kill him, then why haven't you pulled that trigger?" Jackson nodded toward the gun.

Black chuckled. "You were always a smart one, Jacks. That's what I liked about you."

"We all have our strengths," Jackson said casually. He was waiting for Black to let him in on what was brewing behind his calculating eyes. "I'm sure you are well aware of the fact that Stodden had intercepted our hardware source."

Black nodded as he interlaced his fingers and leaned his elbows on his desk. "I'm listening."

"We need guns. We can't exactly parade in and take down John with police issued weapons. I need access to supplies and I will guarantee that I take down Stodden."

Black leaned back in his chair silently. "Stodden is the reason you are fucking caged in this small, filthy section of the city begging for scraps. With him out of the picture you know what that means. What do you have to lose? If I fail, then I'm fucking dead anyway."

"I like these odds." Black scratched his chin. "I can get you some assault rifles and semi-automatic pistols at street tag price."

"What about a sniper, grenades, and vests?" Jackson asked. "I also need lots of ammunition."

"It would take me a day or so but I can get my hands on them. Though, I will need some assurance from you," Black said.

Jackson raised his hands. "What do you have in mind?"

"One of your men."

Jackson shook his head. "I need my men to pull this off."

"I need a reason not to pull this trigger," Black responded as he picked up the gun.

Jackson took a deep breath. "Where do we make the exchange?"

"I'll call you tomorrow when I have the product," Black said, opening his drawer and returning the piece inside. "Don't fucking try to pull any shit, Jackson, or I will reunite you with my knife collection the next time we meet, and I promise you I will do more than just cut off your fucking fingers."

"Fair enough." Jackson pushed off the arms of the chair and stood up. "Who was the winning family of that piece of shit, anyway?" Jackson asked about Seth.

"Turns out Mayor Masten's daddy had a sweet tooth for high school girls. He got one of them pregnant and it became the family's dirty little secret. They paid a shit load of money over the years to keep him alive and off the family tree."

"A family like the Mastens has more than one secret, if you ask me," Jackson replied. The Masten family had been in power a long time and there were always rumblings of something amiss, but their fortune kept their faces clean in the eyes of the public.

"Don't we all."

"What are you gonna tell Masten about his brother?" Jackson asked curiously.

"That I wasn't the one that pulled the fucking trigger. Watch your back," Black warned.

"Always do."

CHAPTER FIFTEEN

Stephanie

Stephanie knew there was something she was supposed to remember. She knew it was important because she could still hear the echo of her racing heart beating loudly in warning, but she couldn't remember why. Her mind was cloudy as she tried to piece her thoughts together. It felt like something was torn away and she was scrambling to fill in the hole left in its place.

A buzzing sound twisted its way into her mind, a sound she couldn't place. Then feeling started to return to her body and a stinging pain appeared against her neck. Stephanie tried to move her head but it felt too heavy. She tried to open her eyes but it was a battle she didn't know if she could win. Her body wanted to submit to unconsciousness but her mind began to reel with potential dangers.

A scratching sensation made a whisper of a moan escape her uncooperative lips. Her body started to thaw and she forced her eyes open.

"Don't move," he ordered.

Stephanie let a strangled cry bubble up her throat when she looked into his face. She felt her foggy senses rush to clarity and she was hit with reality like jumping into cold water. She remembered he had drugged her again. Stephanie tried to move but her arms and legs were bound. When she tried to lift her head, she realized her head was strapped down as well.

"What?" Stephanie managed to say through her quivering lips. "What are you doing?"

"Everything is almost perfect." He smiled down at her as light glared around his shaded face. Stephanie could barely keep her eyes open because the light was too bright from the lamp positioned overhead.

She noticed a tool in his hand and the buzzing sound began to make sense. "Please stop."

"It's almost done. It took me a long time to get the petals just right. Most of the others refused to cooperate and it just didn't look right. It has to be exactly the same or it just doesn't work."

"The others?" Stephanie let the question leave her lips with a sob.

"Don't worry. They're gone. I made sure of it. It's just you and me." He ran his fingers along her cheek, making her stomach twist painfully. "Now don't move or I'll have to drug you again." Stephanie closed her eyes and tried to ignore the pain on her neck. She feared the truth of knowing how many others had endured this before her. How many poor women he abducted from their families and locked away. She tried not to think about where they were now and the fact that she would most likely end up in the same place when he finally realized she was not this Rose girl he imagined her to be.

Stephanie noticed a flash of white in the corner of her eye. She strained to see but the restraints keep her head immobile. Stephanie knew it was the drugs toying with her, she could feel the familiar chill flash across her skin. The drugs always made her hallucinate. Soon she could hear distant cries and they began to drown out the sound of the tattoo machine. They surrounded her like a warning. Something cold brushed against her arm and slowly moved up until it felt like someone had placed their hand on her shoulder. All the hairs on her skin stood on end.

Stephanie tried to shake off the sensation and closed her eyes tight, but the images of countless female faces assaulted her. She hadn't even realized the sound of the tattoo machine had stopped. The only thing she could think about was their faces, all those women whose cries continued to echo in her ear. She pulled against the restraints but they only dug into her flesh, reminding her there was no escape.

She could hear him stop moving. The room became painfully quiet. His face finally came into view and blocked out some of the light.

"I won't let it happen again. I know it made you sad and that's why you had to leave for a while. This time is different. Nothing will come between us."

Tears flooded her vision and she felt them trail

down the sides of her face. He brushed them away with a stroke of his fingers. She had no idea what he was talking about but it didn't make the fear any less potent.

"Don't cry. It makes me hard," he whispered close to her face.

Stephanie gasped and tried to stop her tears but they burned too hot with her fear as they continued to flow. She closed her eyes and tried to calm herself.

"It's been so long since I've been inside you, Rose, but we need to wait until your injection can take effect. We can't have you pregnant again. Not after what happened last time. I thought I lost you for good."

Stephanie felt his fingers brush along her neck and then he closed his hand around her throat, just firm enough to cause her alarm. Her eyes flashed open and she saw him staring at the raw portion of her neck that she could only assume was now covered with a tattoo of some kind. A dark hunger flared in his eyes that made Stephanie hold her breath in terror. He grabbed for his belt buckle with his free hand and unfastened his pants. Stephanie cried out when he pushed his pants down and released his erection. She couldn't stop the tears. They fell freely as she pleaded for him to stop.

He stroked himself as she cried, slowly at first until he became frantic as he stared at her tattoo. Stephanie squeezed her eyes shut, trying to distract her mind from what he was doing but his grunts were harsh reminders of how sick this man really was. His hand against her throat jerked with his movements and made it hard to breathe. Finally he growled out in release and lessened his hold.

Stephanie refused to open her eyes until she heard him refasten his pants. When she did he was looking down at her. His breath was still labored and his eyes were deep, black pools that did not look human.

"Soon, my Rose, soon," he said as he leant down to brush his lips against her forehead. Stephanie's stomach filled with anguish.

CHAPTER SIXTEEN

Lexie

The door to Lexie's room swung open and smashed against the side wall. Lexie knew exactly who it was as she jumped up from the chair. Grabbing her robe ties, she pulled as tight as she could manage. She was wearing a night dress underneath but she wanted as many barriers as she could against Flint. She never wanted him to touch her again. She had turned the shower as hot as she could manage to numb her skin. She wanted to forget the feel of him on her but she couldn't. Now that Jackson knew where she was, she hoped she wouldn't need to try and manipulate Flint anymore. It was too taxing to put herself in that position.

She knew he would be angry, but she didn't expect to see such raging fire behind his dark eyes.

"Where is it?" he demanded. His tie was pulled loose and hung haphazardly around his neck. The top three buttons on his shirt were undone and there was lipstick marks on his neck. The sight brought relief to Lexie because he sought out release with someone else. She would only have to deal with his anger, something she could handle.

"Where's what?" Lexie feigned innocence.

"Don't lie to me." Flint narrowed his eyes. "Tell me where it is now."

Lexie shook her head. "I don't know what you're talking about.

"I know you took my phone. That little scene," Flint said, pointing to the bed. "You managed to get your hands on my phone when I was distracted, didn't you?"

Lexie stepped back as far as she could, rounding to the back of the chair. "I didn't take your phone, Flint. Please stop. You're scaring me."

Flint grabbed hold of the blankets and stripped them from the bed violently and tossed the pillows across the room. Once the bed was bare, he overturned the mattress. When his frantic search ended with nothing, he angrily kicked the bed with a growl. "Tell me where it is or I will tear this whole place apart."

"Go for it." Lexie waved her hands outward. He moved to her dresser and began to pull open all the drawers and grab the clothes and tossed them on the floor. When he didn't find what he was looking for, he headed into the bathroom. Lexie listened as he ransacked her bathroom. She watched a tube of lipstick roll out the doorway. He stepped back out of the bathroom, his eyes skimming the entire room to make sure he didn't miss any place she could have hidden it.

He looked at Lexie for a moment with a clenched

143

jaw. His anger was still potent in his expression as he stalked toward her. She backed against the wall as he grabbed her and searched her. He ran his hands over her robe before he grabbed at the ties. "Stop! I told you I don't have it," Lexie cried out as she shoved him away.

"What's going on in here?" Lexie was relieved to see Miller standing in the open doorway to her room. "Flint?" he questioned.

"Leave us alone, Miller," Flint said sloppily, showcasing the fact that he was drunk.

"He thinks I stole his phone," Lexie explained. "I don't have it."

Miller sighed and came into the room. "Flint, come on. She says she didn't take your phone. Maybe you just dropped it somewhere."

Flint swung around and narrowed his eyes. "Of course you would take her side. You were probably in on this with her," Flint accused. "What did she promise you? Did she tell you that you could fuck her?" Flint turned back to Lexie and grabbed her by the throat. "Did you let him touch you?" Flint's sour breath filled the air.

Lexie tried to say no but he was squeezing her neck too tight. She clawed at his hands and tried to drive her knee into him but he pressed his body against hers. She had no way of gaining leverage.

"Let her go, Flint." Miller approached. Lexie tried to warn Miller when she saw Flint reach for his gun but she could barely make a sound. Miller caught her panicked expression and tried to reach for his weapon but it was too late. Flint already had his hand on the trigger as he turned his body and pulled the trigger.

Flint released her and she fell to the ground. A scream tore through her throat as she looked at Miller. Flint's bullet had hit him next to his eye and the torn remains of his face stared back at her before his body collapsed to the floor and blood began to pool around his head.

Lexie scrambled toward him, knowing full well that the shot was fatal but all she could think about was the fact that he was the only sane person in this entire building. The only one who had shown an ounce of humanity, and now he was gone. She didn't know him well, but she felt the loss of a soul taken too soon.

"What did you do?" Lexie gasped. She looked up at Flint to see him staring at her. It didn't even faze him that he'd just killed a man. He grabbed her by the shoulder and hauled her to her feet. He shoved the barrel of his gun under Lexie's chin and looked down at her with wild bloodshot eyes. A strangled sound escaped her as he pressed the cold metal into the sensitive skin of her throat.

"I want my phone, Lexie."

Lexie flinched from the pain. "I told you I don't have it," she gasped.

Lexie knew there was no way that she would admit that she took it. She would not be the one to sabotage any chance that she and her mother would get out of here. Jackson was her only hope and she couldn't let Flint know that she was in touch with anyone.

Lexie could feel hurried steps coming down the hallway. Flint looked toward the door before he released her, shoving her toward the bed. Lexie landed on the bed and scrambled to the other side and backed up against the wall. She wanted to be as far away as she could from Flint.

A couple of John's men came into the room with their guns raised as they took in the scene.

"What's going on, Flint?" Rayner asked. Surveying the room, he looked down at Miller's body. "Shit, is that Miller?" he asked. He glanced over at Lexie, and then back to Flint, looking for answers.

"Yeah." Flint tucked his gun back into his holster and ran his hands through his hair. "He attacked Lexie. I had to take him out."

"What the fuck is going on in here?" John's voice boomed from the entrance of the room. He walked past Rayner and the other man. He looked around the room and noticed Lexie against the wall and Flint standing near Miller's dead body. "Flint?"

Flint nodded toward Miller's body. "I had no choice."

"Jesus Christ." John rubbed his hand down his face. "Send someone in to clean this mess up and make sure Lexie stays put." John ordered Rayner. "Flint, you come with me." John turned on his heel and walked out of the room.

Flint threw Lexie an accusatory look before he followed John from the room, leaving her feeling terrified of what would happen the next time he came looking for her. He seemed not to want John to know that he believed she had taken his phone, so it bought her some time. But she had nowhere to hide. Lexie prayed that Jackson would come before

Flint took too much from her or John finally revealed his plans for her, though John currently seemed to be the lesser of two evils.

Lexie didn't move as Rayner stood staring at her, still pressed against the wall. She watched two men carry Miller's body out of the room after they had wrapped him in what looked to be a tarp. They acted as if they were dealing with furniture as they covered and taped him. They had no remorse for the man that had just lost his life. She didn't understand how they could be so careless with a man that had worked alongside them. She had only known Miller very briefly but she knew he deserved better than this. She prayed his uncle would show him respect.

"Where are they taking him?" Lexie asked they carried him from the room. She couldn't pull her eyes away from the bloodstain on the floor.

"Away," he grunted. She guessed babysitting her was the last thing he wanted to do.

Rayner pulled out his phone and dialed. He seemed a little unsure of what to do with her, like she would suddenly spontaneously combust. "Send up some cleaners to room 324 and tell them to bring their scrub brushes." He didn't wait for anyone to respond as he disconnected the call and slid his phone back into his pocket.

"Can I get some water, please?" Lexie requested when she noticed how dry her mouth felt. Shock had made her numb but her body was feeling the effects.

Rayner sighed before slipping around the corner and into the bathroom. The thought of making a run for it crossed Lexie's mind but she had nowhere to go. John's men were everywhere and she didn't even know which way to run. John had succeeded in making her feel trapped. Even the open door to her room did not give her hope like it once would have. There was too much promise of death hanging heavy in the air and she didn't want her mother or her to be next.

Lexie tried to avoid looking at the bright red stain on the carpet but her attention kept coming back to it. Tears stung her eyes as she thought of Alex. She quickly reeled in her emotions. She couldn't afford to become fragile right now.

Rayner returned with a full glass of water and thrust it into her hands. The water sloshed over the side and the cool water felt refreshing on her overheated skin. "Thank you," Lexie said out of habit. It's not like she expected him to appreciate manners nor did she think he actually deserved them. She brought it up to her lips, desperate to quench her thirst.

It wasn't long before two women entered pushing a cleaning cart. Lexie was relieved for the distraction because she couldn't stand being alone with Rayner. The women set to work tidying the room without questioning the bloodstain or the state of the room. This must not be the first time they'd cleaned up a crime scene. The only thing Lexie could think of was the fact that Miller's murder was being erased before her eyes.

The maid was on her knees scrubbing the carpet with a bucket and sponge. The bubbles frothed pink as she rubbed furiously at the blood. The woman emptied the bucket a few times and added new soap until the bubbles eventually stayed white and the carpet held little evidence of death. Lexie felt like she was in a trance as she watched her room return to its original state before her eyes. There was no way to know anything violent or horrible had happened in these walls.

The two maids never even acknowledged her as they gathered all their supplies and left the room. Rayner was quick to follow, locking the door behind him. Lexie took a deep breath and pushed off the wall. She slowly walked over to the damp carpet and dropped to her knees. Lexie slowly ran her hand over the surface and couldn't help but think about the piece of peppermint gum that he had given her.

"I hope you find peace, Miller," Lexie whispered through her tight throat. She never wanted to get used to people being killed before their time. That was why she could never stay in John's world, even if death was her only way out. She would fight for life even if it meant losing it.

CHAPTER SEVENTEEN

Jackson

Jackson leaned back on the hood of his car. The comforting sound of his music flooded his ears. He needed to calm himself. Knowing where Lexie was being kept made him want to move now, but having to wait until the pieces lined up caused him inner turmoil. If he went after her unprepared it wouldn't do any of them any good. He wasn't surprised anymore by the fact that his focus had shifted from finding out the details behind his father's murder to Lexie. She was all he could think about and it made all the other noise in his head fade away. He was still planning on avenging his father, but it was now secondary to this new desire to set Lexie's life straight. He couldn't get her image out of his head, or the desire to physically hold her to know she was safe.

Jackson was lying to himself when he thought he could walk away from her once he brought her home. With every passing second his feelings for her wove deeper and deeper into his very being. Whatever the future held for him, he had come to believe it would bring only pain, but it was a truth he had already accepted. The only thing for certain was that he refused to take his last breath until John Stodden was dead and Rosh was exposed for his part in his father's death. Rosh may have pulled the trigger but he knew John was behind the order.

The heat of the sun on his face almost gave him the illusion that he was comfortable, but the truth of the situation sat like a rock in his stomach. Someone nudged Jackson's shoulder and he opened his eyes to see Teddy pointing toward two approaching vehicles. He pulled the earbuds from his ears and sat up.

He glanced around to see Dane throwing rocks at a nearby sign. The repetitive sound of impact rang out over and over again with each successful hit. "Dane? Where's Evan?" Jackson called out, not seeing him anywhere.

Dane spun around and pointed toward the line of trees behind them. "He went to take a leak." Dane dropped the rest of the rocks and wiped his hands off on his pants before he headed back toward the car.

The unmarked van and car pulled up to a stop several yards away and kicked up a cloud of dust in the abandoned parking lot of an old industrial building. Jackson remembered it as an old shoe factory years ago before it shut down and was left to deteriorate. The doors were boarded and a few windows were broken. Someone had even gotten creative with a can of spray paint and tagged the building with questionable art.

The side door of the van slid open. Two men stepped out of the back and stood guard on either side of the door. Slash stepped out of his car and rounded the vehicle. Jackson wasn't surprised to see him. He'd always had a personal vendetta against Jackson. "I'd say I'm sorry we're late but I'm not," Slash said arrogantly as he walked closer to Jackson.

"I can see that," Jackson said, pushing off the car with his foot. He picked up the bag between his feet and tossed it toward Slash. It landed in front of his feet. "It's all there." Jackson waved with his hand. Slash looked down at the bag and extracted his knife from his pocket. He flipped it open, crouched down, and used the knife's tip to hook the zipper and pull the bag open. He did a quick survey of the stacks before he closed the bag and stood up. "Impressive for a cop's salary."

"I'm a good saver." Jackson smirked. "Let's see the guns." He nodded toward the van. The two men standing guard pulled two large bags out of the back and carried them over toward Jackson and dropped them on the ground. When they opened the bags, they revealed the guns as Black had promised. Jackson did a quick survey to make sure all the inventory was accounted for.

Dane's eyes lit up. "And I thought you didn't get me anything," Dane said with a smile. He knelt down slowly and pulled the sniper rifle out of the bag. "An M24. I take back all the bad things I said about you."

"I knew you'd like it better than flowers,"

Jackson said.

"Fuck flowers." Dane examined the gun with an appreciative expression. "I have a hard on right now."

"What's wrong with him?" Slash waved his hand at Dane, who used the car to help himself to his feet. It wasn't hard to tell that he was injured.

"He got shot," Jackson said casually with a dismissive wave of his hand.

"Yeah, he was jerking off with his gun again," Teddy said with a laugh as he smacked Dane on the back. "Kids these days don't learn."

"Don't judge, we all have our weaknesses," Dane said, completely straight-faced as he looked through the scope of the rifle.

Slash raised his brow as he looked at Jackson. "Is he the one we're taking?"

Dane lowered the gun and Teddy swung around to look at Jackson. "What is he talking about, Jacks?" Teddy asked.

Jackson scratched the back of his neck. "Black asked for one of you to stay with him for collateral." Jackson should have mentioned this to the guys before now but he knew that Evan would not cooperate with the plan if he was given a heads-up. Jackson needed this plan to happen if they were going to succeed. Jackson turned around and found Evan standing quietly behind them. He already had a suspicious look on his face when he looked back at Jackson.

"Let me guess…' Evan said flatly.

Jackson walked over toward him and grabbed him by the shoulder, walking him a few more steps

153

away to speak in private. Dane and Teddy followed him, insistent on being part of the conversation. "Black asked for insurance that we would follow through. At least this time no one is going to beat the shit out of you unless you do something to deserve it." Jackson tried to make the situation seem lighter. He looked back over his shoulder at Slash, who seemed to be growing restless. Evan shook his head in disbelief.

"You know I need Dane and Ted with me if I'm going to pull this off. Think of Lexie, Stephanie, and her mother. Think of it as a little vacation where you get to hang around a strip bar for a day or two until we get the girls back," Jackson argued his point.

"Fuck…Jackson, I hate you," Evan growled, raking his hands down his face.

"Just stay away from the smack or whatever they're passing around and you'll be fine, baby bro. Maybe you'll get your first blow job." Teddy patted Evan on the side of the face.

Evan threw him a dirty look before he shoved his hand away. "Are you ever fucking serious, Teddy?"

"Listen, Evan." Jackson waited for Evan to look at him before he continued. "I promise we won't leave you there. We came for you last time, didn't we?"

"If they kill me, Jackson, I will haunt you every day for the rest of your fucking life."

"Fine, but they aren't going to hurt you," Jackson assured him. "Black gave me his word you would be treated like a guest."

"Unless we don't kill John," Dane added with a

quick tilt of his head. All three of them glared at Dane. "Just sayin'." Dane shrugged before he walked back toward the guns.

"It'll be fine, and before you know it we'll have the girls back." Jackson grabbed Evan by the shoulder but Evan jerked away and took a few steps back.

"You better be right." Evan glared at him. "When this is all over I don't want to see any of you again."

Teddy placed his hand over his heart. "That's a bit dramatic, don't you think? What am I gonna tell Mom?"

"Oh, by the way, that guy from Seth's house that you let leave is lurking in the trees. He said he needs to talk to you," Evan said angrily.

"Shit." Jackson rubbed the back of his neck. "Okay."

Let's get this over with." Evan started toward the van but then stopped and turned around to face Jackson. "Oh, just one more thing." Evan wound up and punched Jackson in the face. Jackson saw it coming but he allowed him to get this one in. He deserved it.

Jackson licked his lip and spit blood out of his mouth. "Are you done?" he asked, wiping his busted lip with the back of his hand. "If you ever do that again I will kill you."

"Holy shit…that made me feel so much better," Evan said, shaking the pain out of his hand. "Make sure you bring them home," Evan said before walking toward the others.

"Little brother is growing up," Teddy said as he

wrapped his arm around Jackson's shoulder. Jackson looked at Teddy and sighed before he followed Evan.

"It's all there," Dane said when Jackson walked up beside him. "We're all ready for the party now." Dane rubbed his hands together excitedly.

"Jackson." Slash walked up to them. He continuously flipped his knife open and closed. It was his art of intimidation that he had mastered over the years but the effect was lost on Jackson. He knew Slash was just a lunatic with a knife. "What makes you think that you can take down Stodden when no one else can?"

Jackson clenched his jaw and looked up at Slash. "Because I have really big balls," he said. Teddy erupted into laughter behind him.

Slash raised his brow in irritation. "Well, when you fail, I'll enjoy cutting them off you." Slash smiled sadistically. He flipped his knife up into the air and caught it before he slipped it into his pocket.

"I bet you would," Dane mumbled under his breath.

Slash glanced at Dane before turning his attention back toward Jackson. "We'll be hearing from you soon," Slash demanded.

Evan climbed into the back of the van without a backward glance. Jackson knew he wasn't happy with them, but his part was as necessary as theirs. As much as Evan irritated him, he wouldn't let him be put in unnecessary danger.

Jackson watched the men pile back into the vehicles and drive away. Their wheels kicked up a wall of dust as they drove away.

"I think I might actually miss that little fucker," Teddy said with a frown.

Jackson was watching the van disappear when his phone began to ring. He looked at the screen to see Giles' name.

"It's Giles, isn't it?" Teddy asked, looking at Jackson's expression.

"Yeah." Jackson ignored the call. By now Giles would know what Jackson was up to but they just needed a bit more time to pull this off.

Teddy's phone started ringing immediately after. "Don't answer it. We need to get to work. We'll deal with Giles after the shit hits the fan," Jackson said as he headed toward the treeline. Teddy was close on his heels.

Jackson pulled his gun from his holster. "Come out, Nate," Jackson hollered. He didn't know what his intentions were, but he knew that if he tried anything, he would be ready.

Nate walked toward them with his hands raised. "I just want to talk, Jackson," Nate said as he stepped into view. Jackson stared at him over the barrel of his gun, unsure if he should trust him or not. A long time had passed and he wasn't sure if he was the same person he once knew.

Jackson dropped his gun. "What do you want?"

Nate lowered his hands and walked closer. Teddy still seemed unsure and didn't put his guard down. Nate threw Teddy a wary glance as he came to stand a few feet away from Jackson. "I just want to talk to you, man."

"It's all right, Teddy." Jackson nodded. Teddy reluctantly lowered his gun but didn't put it away.

"You just left without a word," Nate said dejectedly as he ran his hand through his hair. "I was so fucking mad at you for leaving. You were all I had and you knew it."

"I didn't have a choice, Nate," Jackson said. "I sent someone to find you but they said you were gone."

"Yeah, I had no reason to stay." Nate bit the inside of his cheek thoughtfully as he looked at Jackson. There was so much emotion in his eyes Jackson couldn't help but feel it. "I ratted on you to save my ass. I knew Black was ready to kick me to the curb, but Seth, he was looking for a reason to hate you and I gave it to him. I didn't think you were ever coming back."

Jackson stared into the eyes of the one person who truly knew what he had to endure on the streets. Nate had been by his side through most of it. They had both done many things that would haunt then for the rest of their days.

"You saved my ass so many times and I know I can never really pay you back, but I want to try," Nate said.

"Nate..." Jackson started.

"I want to help you. I owe you that."

Jackson began to shake his head.

"I need to do this, Jackson," Nate said.

Jackson turned around and looked at Teddy and Dane, who were both watching the exchange.

"Seriously, Jacks," Dane said, shaking his head.

CHAPTER EIGHTEEN

Evan

The van pulled into the same parking garage as they were brought to the day before. The two men Evan had the luxury of riding with filed out of the side door before ordering him to follow. He didn't expect any hospitality but he could have definitely done without the glares they insisted on giving him the entire drive. Evan jumped out of the van and was immediately ushered through the back entrance of the club.

The seductive music vibrated through his feet as he walked into the dim lighting. He was surprised to see the bar in full swing so early in the afternoon. Though the dancing seemed to be slightly tamer and relaxed compared to night before, the crowd had already begun to form.

Evan was led toward one of the many designated bar sections. This one was tucked away in the back corner and mostly deserted except for one lone customer slumped against the bar and the bartender

159

stacking glasses. "Sit down," the man Evan thought resembled a bulldog ordered as he pointed toward the stool on the end of the bar.

"Since you asked so nicely," Evan replied as he dropped down in the seat. Bulldog leaned over him. "What the hell, man." Evan looked down and realized he had handcuffed him to the metal rail that ran along the edge of the bar top. "Oh come on, seriously?" Evan pulled against the cuff, making the metal clank loudly against the bar.

"Seriously," Bulldog growled. "Now stay put."

"Like I have a choice." Evan rattled the cuffs. "You don't think this will raise any flags? There are customers all over the place." Evan pointed toward the man at the end of the bar that actually looked like he might be passed out. "Well, maybe not him, but anyone can walk by."

"We're in a strip bar, man. Cuffs are part of the package," Bulldog said, waving his hands.

Evan nodded in agreement. "What the fuck ever. Guess it's not the worst thing that has happened to me lately." Evan sighed and leaned against the bar.

"Watch him," Bulldog ordered the bartender before he stalked away.

"You look like you need a drink. Let me guess, you're a beer guy?" The bartender slid a beer in front of him.

Evan looked up and noticed for the first time that the female bartender didn't look so female upon closer inspection. "Whoa, are you a dude?" Evan asked before he thought better of it.

"Ding, ding, ding, we have a genius in our midst, people." The bartender turned toward the passed out man at the end of the bar. "Did you hear that, Jimmy? This guy figured me right the fuck out and I thought I had everyone fooled." The man at the end of the bar gave a grunt and a small wave of his hand.

"Sorry, you just caught me off guard," Evan said apologetically.

"And you are a green motherfucker from a small town, aren't you?" The bartender placed her hands on her hips. "Do you want this beer or not, Sugar?"

"Yes, please." Evan grabbed the beer and greedily tipped it up to his lips. The soothing cold liquid gave him immediate relief. "My name's Evan."

"Your name says it all." The bartender shook her head and sighed. "I'm Cherry, and it looks like you got yourself into some trouble. Didn't I see you here last night with those other hotties that came strolling in here all G.I. Joe style?" Cherry raised her perfectly shaped eyebrow.

"Yeah, don't get me started on that." Evan tipped the beer up to his lips and took a long swallow.

"I thought old Black finally took me up on my suggestion for elephant night around here." Cherry smiled. "A girl can dream." Cherry trailed off before she grabbed Evan's empty bottle off the counter and dropped it in the recycling bin. "Looks like Benny is coming back to collect you."

Evan turned around to see the thick man heading their way. "Benny? He looks more like a Bulldog to me." Evan said with a frown. "He has himself a serious steroid addiction."

"That is one thing we do agree on, Sugar,"

Cherry said as she placed her hand on her hip.

When Benny approached, he awkwardly acknowledged Cherry before he pulled the cuff key out of his pocket and unlocked Evan. "Follow me," he grunted.

"Thanks, Cherry," Evan said, rubbing his wrist. "I'll put in a good word for elephant night."

"Good luck, you're gonna need it," Cherry called out, shaking her head with a smile.

Benny led Evan back toward Black's office. He followed Benny inside Black's spacious room before Benny closed the door behind them. The office was surprisingly not as tacky as he would have thought the owner of a strip bar would have had. There was no sex related décor, or posters. It was tastefully decorated.

"Hello, Evan," Black said, leaning back in his chair. "I'm going to get straight to the point. I don't care to babysit you. You being here just gives me the insurance I need that Jackson will keep his word. I trust that you will quietly wait out your time, but if you try to walk out any of the doors, you will not leave alive. Do you understand me?"

"Yes sir," Evan said with a nod.

"I suggest you blend in and keep a low profile." Black sat up in his chair. "In fact, I don't wish to see you again until Jackson returns. He assured me that you won't cause trouble."

"You won't even know I'm here," Evan confirmed.

"One more thing, Evan." Black made sure he had Evan's full attention. "Keep your dick away from the girls."

Evan raised his hands. "Of course, yeah. I wasn't planning on—"

"Benny will show you where to go," Black said dismissively as he turned his attention back toward his computer screen.

Evan followed Benny out to the hall and into a small private lounge down a long narrow passageway. The room opened up into an area with several seating areas that consisted of sofas and chairs. It was cluttered with what looked like glittery stage attire and the coffee tables were littered with discarded takeout boxes and cups. Evan had never claimed to be neat but even he found the space messy. It looked to also be a prep area for the girls, a row of vanities lined one wall and a few women were touching up their makeup.

Benny gave Evan a shove on the back of the shoulder. "Sit." He pointed toward the nearest sofa.

"What did you bring us, Benny? A snack?" A platinum blonde wearing a red silk robe sauntered over toward them.

"I need you ladies to keep an eye on him while I track down Dillon to watch him," Benny said as he grabbed the cuffs out of his pocket. He grabbed hold of one of the bars covering the window behind the sofa and gave it a shake to confirm it was secure. "Sit," he ordered Evan.

"Again with the cuffs? Can't I just promise not to go anywhere?" Evan asked hopefully.

"Sit," Benny barked impatiently.

Evan dropped down on the sofa with a sigh and held out his hand. Benny grabbed it and secured the cuff around his wrist before fastening him to the metal bars that lined the large window. "Really? This is a bit uncomfortable," Evan complained as he pulled against the restricting angle.

"I'll be back," Benny said before storming off.

"What if I have to go to the washroom?" Benny ignored him. "Fuck!" Evan said in annoyance as he gave his arm a shake against the cuffs. "He's full of personality, isn't he?" The girls in the room were all watching him curiously.

"Yeah, Benny can be a bit much, sometimes." The platinum blonde smiled and walked over to sit beside him. She placed her hand on his thigh and leaned in. "So what's your story?"

"Ah..." Evan leaned back into the sofa. He was taken aback by her forwardness. "I'm just fulfilling a lifelong dream of being handcuffed in a strip bar." He answered with the first thing that came to mind. He didn't think it wise to get into any truthful details.

She giggled at his answer and bit her lip. "You're funny. I like you." She ran her hand up his thigh and Evan became very still.

"I like you too and I also like that robe," Evan said, letting his gaze drop to the front, where the silky fabric barely covered her breasts. "Red is a good color on you." Evan's voice cracked and he cleared his throat to hide the fact that she made him very nervous.

"You're sweet." She placed a kiss on his cheek.

A woman leaned in the doorway. "Krystal, you're up." Her long chestnut hair was pulled back into a high ponytail. She wore nothing but bright sparkly blue underwear. Evan tried to keep his gaze respectful but he was overwhelmed by all the exposed flesh.

"I gotta go, sweetheart. I'll be back to check on you later." Krystal patted his leg and pushed off the sofa.

"Who's this?" the brunette asked curiously as she pointed at Evan.

Krystal shrugged her shoulders. "Benny dropped him off."

"Evan," he offered his name. "Nice to meet you."

"Yes, it is." The brunette winked and followed Krystal down the hallway.

Evan tried to adjust his arm but it didn't do any good. He leaned back on the sofa and watched the girls primping across the room. He hoped Jackson knew what he was doing. Evan felt anxious having to wait around, not knowing what was happening.

Evan was starting to feel himself drift to sleep when the door slammed closed and he bolted up in his seat. A sharp pain pulled at his arm from being held at an odd angle. He moaned in distress as he looked up to see Krystal staring down at him. "You scared the shit out of me." He threw his arm over his face and tried to adjust his arm.

"Do you want to party with me?" Krystal asked. The closeness of her voice startled him and he opened his eyes to see her leaning in.

He raised his brow and rattled his cuff to remind her that he was in no position to party. She crawled onto his lap and Evan looked around the room to see they were alone. He narrowed his eyes in question.

She grabbed the ties of her robe and pulled it open, baring her breasts. "Whoa." Evan gasped, his hesitance slipping away. It was hard to think logically when a naked woman was sitting on his lap.

Krystal reached into her panties and pulled out a small packet of pills. "What're those?" Evan asked as she opened them.

"A little something to take the edge off," she said excitedly.

Evan looked at the pills she held up to his mouth. "I really shouldn't," Evan said as she placed it against his lips.

"Open up," she cooed.

"I'm a recovering..." Evan leaned back in his seat and stared up at the ceiling in disbelief. How could he say no when a naked woman was trying to feed him Percocet? The last week of misery faded from his mind as he fought to get himself clean. All he could think about was the immediate relief the drug could give him and the erection straining in his pants. "Fuck it. Give it to me." Evan opened his mouth and a wide smile brightened her face. She leaned back and grabbed a glass off the table and held it up for him to take.

He brought it to his lips and sipped the cheap whiskey that burned his mouth and throat, but he didn't care. He wanted to forget where he was as he downed the entire glass. He closed his eyes and leaned back against the sofa. Krystal leaned in and kissed his neck, pressing her body against his.

"I have a thing for men in handcuffs," Krystal whispered against his ear.

"I've noticed." Evan smiled lazily. The combination of the pills and the liquor were starting to burn away the edges of his reality and he welcomed it with open arms. "Do you have anymore?" Evan asked. He tilted his head up to meet her lips.

"Of course." She passed him the package. Evan tipped it up to his mouth and swallowed a few more before he grabbed her by the back of the head and deepened the kiss.

CHAPTER NINETEEN

Jackson

"Did you take too many painkillers? What the fuck is wrong with you?" Teddy swatted the flower that Dane was tickling his neck with. "I'm trying to work here."

"Just trying to show you how annoying you can be," Dane said with a laugh. "How's it feel to be on the receiving end?"

"Well, I'm glad I don't have to put up with me," Teddy said as he typed away on his computer. They were in the back of a floral cargo van that Teddy had acquired to allow them access to the hotel without drawing attention. The local flower shop was down the street from hotel and shouldn't be cause for concern if seen near the location. Jackson had put Teddy in charge of attaining a vehicle and he did not disappoint. Jackson didn't want to rent anything because it would raise flags to those who might be keeping an eye on his activity.

"How did you even talk that woman into giving

you this van, anyway?" Jackson asked, leaning back through the front seats.

"Why do you guys always doubt my skills?" Teddy said, shaking his head.

"We're just amazed that people fall for your shit," Jackson said as he smiled at Dane.

"Did you sleep with her?" Dane asked suspiciously.

"No, I'm not like that." Teddy tried to keep a straight face but ended up laughing. "But seriously, I didn't sleep with her."

"You feeling all right?" Dane asked with narrowed eyes as he put his hand on Teddy's forehead. Teddy pulled away from him.

"It's that girl from the apartment," Jackson said. "He's all shook up." He laughed.

"I felt like that the first time I saw tits too," Dane teased.

"I know you two are bored as I do my thing, but seriously, I'm trying to infiltrate a fucking fortress here," Teddy said firmly as he waved at his computer.

"Yeah, yeah, don't cry," Dane said as he crawled through the front seats and dropped down in the passenger seat next to Jackson.

"And don't go thinking I'm in love or some foolish shit like that. I don't do love," Teddy called out.

"Whatever, lover boy," Dane teased. He stretched out his legs and got comfortable. "How are ya, man?" Dane turned his head and looked over at Jackson.

"Trying not to think about it," Jackson answered

truthfully. He stared out at the dark street stretched out before them. They were parked on a deserted dirt road a short walk through the trees to the hotel that bordered on the edge of Sugar Hill. A thick green belt stretched far off into the distance. The landscape gave them lots of opportunity to get on the property undetected. They just needed to override the security system and gain access to the power grid of the hotel, the two things that Teddy was currently working on.

"We'll get her back, Jacks," Dane said as he stared off into the landscape. "And we'll make that fucker pay."

Jackson turned his head and looked at Dane. Somehow along the way the three of them had created a bond they depended on, they had become family. Jackson's phone lit up in the console with Giles' number. He had been calling all day. They both watched the screen until it went black.

"How long do you think it took Giles to figure out Teddy made our phones untraceable?"

"I guarantee that's the first thing he tried when he found out we weren't still at the Belhaven Precinct. So not long," Jackson said, closing his eyes. He was putting everything he had into taking down Stodden. He was leading Dane and Teddy into the storm and he hoped they would all be able to walk away.

Jackson had always tested the boundaries and bent the rules but this was different. This was going beyond anything he had ever done and he wasn't sure what would happen when or if he faced Giles.

"I'm in," Teddy said triumphantly. They both

turned around to see Teddy typing away, his face aglow from the screen in the otherwise darkened interior. "I just have to link this up to my phone and we should be a go."

A set of headlights lit up the interior as a car passed, turned around, and pulled up in front of their vehicle.

"Do you really think we can trust him, Jacks?" Dane asked.

"I believe so," Jackson answered. He opened the window when he saw Nate approach.

Nate grabbed the top of the door as he leaned in the open window. "Floors two through four are blocked off for extensive renovations. I booked a room on the fifth floor and the main elevators don't even stop on those floors. They must have their own private elevator."

"What about security?"

"As far as I can tell, it's operating like a normal hotel. Nothing else appears to be out of the ordinary. I didn't notice any suspicious vehicles in the parking lot, but there appears to be an underground parking garage only for hotel staff. They could be using that. I took a picture of the access panel."

Jackson took Nate's phone and flipped through the pictures he took of the hotel and exterior. "You sure no one saw you?" Jackson looked up to see Nate's face lit by the light of the phone. He was older now but still the same as Jackson remembered.

"No, man. All good."

"Good." Jackson passed Nate's phone back

between the seats. "What do you think of this, Ted?"

Teddy took the phone and flipped through the pictures. "It's a standard code entry lock, shouldn't be a problem. That's probably our best entry point."

Jackson opened the door and walked around to the back of the van. He opened the back to retrieve the car jack they had stashed with their supplies. "What do you want me to do?" Nate asked.

"You can stay with the van." Jackson placed the jack under the van and secured it under the driver's side rear. Dane grabbed a socket and unscrewed the hub cap off the wheel and placed a few road cones on the edge of the road to make anyone driving by dismiss it as a vehicle with a flat tire.

Jackson unzipped the large duffle bag in the back and began arming himself with supplies.

"You sure you don't need an extra man?" Nate asked eagerly.

"You would be more help here, keeping an eye on the outside for us," Jackson said as he tucked an earbud in his ear and grabbed his M16 assault rifle. Teddy hopped out of the back and swung his backpack over his shoulder.

"All set," Teddy said, taking the rifle Dane held out for him.

"I hope you know what you're doing," Nate said, leaning against the side of the van.

"Still the worrier, I see." Jackson raised his brow.

"Some things never change." Nate nodded toward Jackson. "You're still doing crazy, dangerous shit. Are you seriously only taking two guys with you to take down a fucking giant?"

"We have explosives. What more do we need?" Teddy laughed.

Jackson placed his hand on Nate's shoulder. "Just stay with the van."

Nate nodded and crossed his arms. "Yeah, okay."

Jackson shut the doors. "Ready?" Jackson asked Teddy and Dane.

"Yeah, let's go," Dane said, heading toward the trees, his guns strapped over his shoulder.

"Good luck," Nate said as Jackson turned to follow.

"Don't believe in luck," Jackson replied. "You know that."

"Maybe you should," Nate added.

Jackson ducked into the trees and headed through the dark landscape that led to the hotel property. Jackson took the lead as he navigated over the short distance of rough terrain until the trees started to thin and the lights of the property shone through. He signaled them to stop and retrieved his binoculars to scan the perimeter.

Dane knelt down and found a place to set up his sniper rifle. "Where are the cameras, Teddy?" Jackson whispered.

Teddy pulled out his laptop. "We have one over the parking garage entrance and over the fire escape."

"What about the roof?" Jackson said, looking up.

"Nothing," Teddy responded after a moment clicking away on his screen.

"I've have a visual of at least two bodies on the

roof, Jacks. I can't tell if they're armed or not from this angle," Dane said, looking through the scope of his gun.

"Hold off until we have confirmation they're Stodden's men," Jackson said. Something caught his attention in his peripheral view. "We have an incoming vehicle," Jackson watched the black SUV approach. The vehicle came around the side of the building and pulled up to the parking garage entrance. Jackson trained his binoculars on the driver's side window as it lowered for the driver to enter the code.

"And we have a winner," Jackson said, recognizing the man behind the wheel as one of the men in John's circle. "Nate was right about the parking garage."

"The men on the roof are targets," Dane announced after he confirmed they were armed.

"How about a little noise distraction, Teddy?" Jackson asked.

"Coming right up," Teddy announced wickedly. "I got just the thing to set the mood."

In a matter of minutes, multiple car alarms erupted from the parking lot. "Nice," Jackson said. "Dane, you're up next. Clear our path."

They all grew quiet as Dane set his sights on his targets. He shot the first round off, then quickly cocked the gun, and followed with the second. Jackson watched both men drop before they had a chance to register what happened.

"Let's move," Jackson said, heading toward the side of the hotel. Raising his gun, he shot out the light over the parking garage door to give them more cover before he broke free of the treeline. Jackson took cover against the side of the building, trying to stay out of sight. Teddy and Dane were close on his heels, coming up next to him.

"You're up, Teddy," Jackson said, holding his rifle up to cover him.

"Yeah, no pressure," Dane said, pressing his back against the door. "It's not like we're sitting ducks here."

"Hold on," Teddy said as he used his knife to pry open a panel on the front of the key pad. He pulled out a cord and plugged his computer in and started typing. "Got it." Teddy shoved his laptop back in his backpack. The door began to open and they stepped back out of view until they cleared the entrance.

Jackson stepped forward with this gun raised and entered. It looked like a standard hotel parking garage except for the fact that it was mainly vacant. There was only a cluster of vehicles toward the central elevator and the newcomer had already parked and left his vehicle. Teddy had already informed them that all surveillance cameras on the lower floors were offline, which made it easier for them to move around undetected.

Jackson led them toward the stairwell in the far corner of the garage. The only advantage they had was the element of surprise and they intended to take full advantage of it. Stodden's men never hesitated to pull the trigger and Jackson wanted to make sure they kept the upper hand. The weight of this undertaking burned heavy and hot in his stomach.

Jackson relished in the thrill of finally facing the demon who had brought down his father but what he didn't expect was the weight of fear that came with Lexie's captivity. He needed to ensure she was unharmed when the walls came crashing down. Lexie was his taste of light in his dark, twisted world. She was what he would hold in his heart once this battle was over.

Jackson kept his steps light as he ascended the stairwell, the calming music playing low in his ear. Teddy and Dane were only a few steps behind him as he moved quickly. The stairwell door ahead opened and a man's voice began to flood the silence, echoing through the open space. It sounded like he was talking on the phone. Jackson held his hand up to stop Dane and Teddy.

"Yeah, yeah, I'll call you later," the man said. Jackson continued up the stairs by himself. The man was still standing on the landing, scrolling through his phone when Jackson walked up the steps. He looked up when he noticed Jackson and his eyes immediately narrowed. "Who are you?" he asked with a confused expression.

"Let me introduce myself." Jackson smiled as he stepped up on the landing. He reached for his blade.

"Oh shit!" the man called out when Jackson swung it down in a swift motion, impaling the man in the throat. His eyes bulged before he let out a strangled sound and grabbed hold of Jackson's arm as the light drained from his eyes. He collapsed on the ground and a puddle of dark red blood began to pool around him.

"Let's go," Jackson called down toward Dane

and Teddy. He waited for them to meet him before he pulled open the door with his gun raised.

"What the fuck?" a man standing on the other side of the door questioned when he saw Jackson emerge from the stairwell. He was standing with two others in the door of a room off the main hall. Jackson grabbed for the man as he reached for his gun. He twisted his arm back and shoved him into the room. Once inside, Jackson ran his blade across the man's throat and then released him, kicking him into the bathroom. Dane and Teddy were already taking down the other two men, careful to keep the noise level down so to not alert anyone else. They wanted their presence to remain undetected for as long as they could to keep the odds in their favor. They were not certain how many men John had at this location. The men had struggled but were unprepared to defend themselves when taken by surprise. They didn't even have time to retrieve their weapons before they were taken out.

Jackson signalled them to follow when he made sure the hallway was clear. He could hear voices down the hall, coming from another room in the distance. Jackson made his way down the hallway until he came to room 324. The door was modified to have an exterior lock that was left unlatched. Jackson's stomach felt like lead as he turned the handle and swung the door open. He raised his gun and took a cautious step inside. He passed by the bathroom door and pushed it open to reveal it was empty before he continued further into the main part of the room.

Though Lexie was not there he could still smell

her familiar scent, indicating that she had only recently left. He dropped his gun and turned around to face Dane and Teddy. He couldn't hide his disappointment.

"Did you really think it would be that easy?" Dane whispered with his brows raised.

"No, but it would have been nice." Jackson gave the room a quick search. It looked like a typical hotel room. Nothing seemed to be out of place. Teddy opened up the top drawer of the dresser. "At least they're dressing her well," Teddy said, turning around as he held up a lacy pair of underwear.

Jackson shook his head and headed toward the door and peered out into the hall. "Ready?" he asked. "Let's go."

CHAPTER TWENTY

Lexie

Lexie rubbed her forehead. She was exhausted from lying awake the night before, terrified that Flint would return. Every sound had her on edge and it made it impossible for her to sleep. She looked across the desk at John, who was holding another envelope identical to the one she had torn to pieces. He slid it across the surface of the desk so it was sitting in front of her.

"How about this time you just hold onto it until you're ready?" John said as he leaned back and placed his hands on the arms of the chair.

"Why don't you just tell me?" Lexie looked up from the envelope.

"Forcing things on you doesn't seem to work now, does it?" John said, tapping his fingers on the armrests.

"So you're getting to know me after all. I thought that would be impossible since you keep me locked in a room," Lexie responded casually. She didn't have any bite in her words this morning. She was feeling too drained.

"On the contrary, I know you very well," John responded in a manner that made her skin crawl. She desperately wanted to ask where Stephanie was, but to do that she would give up the fact that she has reason to doubt him. Flint was standing behind her and she knew it would solidify the truth he already suspected, she took his phone. She couldn't risk it. She needed to trust that Jackson was coming. John obviously didn't want her to know where Stephanie was or he wouldn't have led her to believe she was safe. She couldn't trust any of these men.

"Where did they take Miller's body?" Lexie asked instead. The image of Miller's lifeless body haunted her thoughts.

"It doesn't matter," John answered coldly. "He's dead."

"You're wrong. It does matter," Lexie said defensively. "He was a good person and didn't deserve to be killed."

John tilted his head. "There is no such thing as a good person, Lexie. Everyone lies, steals, and litters the world."

"No." Lexie shook his head. "He was trying to help me. He should be buried with his mother."

"Miller stepped out of line if your conversations lead toward his personal life. Is this what you so urgently wanted to speak to me about?" John looked impatient as he glanced at his watch.

"No." Lexie turned around and looked at Flint, whose eyes had been burning a hole in her back since she walked into the office. She turned back around to address John. "Can I speak with you privately?"

"John, we have things to—" Flint began.

"Leave us," John cut Flint off and waved him from the room.

Lexie listened to Flint's retreating footsteps before she heard the sound of the door close behind her. She couldn't bear to look at Flint again after what had happened. She looked up at John's calculating gaze and knew she needed to work up the strength to talk to him.

"Flint lied to you," Lexie said apprehensively, playing with the material of her dress. "Miller was trying to help me. It was Flint who attacked me." Lexie prayed she was right in that Flint feared John. She hoped John would see Flint's actions as a betrayal, it was the only play she had left. She watched John clench his jaw as he listened intently. "He was drunk and…" Lexie trailed off when noise erupted outside John's door. Men were shouting and running down the hall.

Lexie spun around when John's door burst open. "We have company," Rayner said. He held his gun in his hand as he peered down the passage.

"Who?" John demanded as he opened his desk drawer and pulled out a pistol.

Rayner's radio attached to his hip began to erupt in a frenzy of voices that Lexie couldn't distinguish. It echoed the noise coming from down the hall. "Don't know."

Fear and excitement roared to life inside Lexie's chest. She desperately wanted it to be Jackson but she also feared what would happen if he didn't succeed. A part of her wanted to believe he was here for her despite knowing the truth of his intentions. It was the part of her that refused to let go of the feelings he stirred deep within her. Her worry for his safety surprised her and made her realize how difficult it would be to hate Jackson.

John rounded his desk, grabbed her arm, and hauled her to her feet. "You're coming with me. Don't try anything," John threatened.

Lexie gasped in surprise as his firm grip dug into her skin as he pulled her toward the door. "Where's Flint?"

"I haven't seen him since earlier," Rayner responded as he looked up and down the hall. "I thought he was with you."

Unsure of what else to do, Lexie let herself be towed along. She didn't know the building well enough to use the distraction to her advantage. She kept her eyes open for exit signs as they moved down the hallway. Her adrenaline pumped through her system as the sounds of chaos and gunfire seemed to be just out of sight and drew closer every second.

Lexie stumbled as they turned a corner but John didn't allow her to slip from his grasp. He hauled her back on her feet, jolting her arm enough to make her eyes water.

When her mother's door came into view, Lexie felt a swell of emotion hit her in the chest. Rayner stepped up to the door and pulled a set of keys from his pocket. When the door swung open, Lexie tried to pull free from John's hold, but he refused to release her. "Let me see her." Lexie tried to pry his hand from her. "Please."

She looked up to see his dark, cold eyes staring down at her. Her struggles immediately died away. His gaze was filled with so much evil it made her sick to her stomach. There was nothing human about the man looking down at her. His other hand snaked up and grabbed her by the throat. He pushed her back against the wall as he asserted his grip on her neck. "Stop fighting me."

Lexie couldn't even manage a sound as he applied pressure and blocked off the ability to speak. All she could do was look into his dark eyes that promised so much pain and death. One of John's men came around the corner. He was walking backward with his gun raised toward anyone that may be following him.

The man Lexie recognized as Jacobs turned to acknowledge John. "They're heading this way."

Rayner's radio flared to life again. The voice that filtered through was familiar and it immediately made her stomach heat with emotions. "I know you're here, Stodden. I'm coming for you."

Lexie managed a strangled gasp through John's grasp. Jacobs began to fire his gun and John pulled her into the room behind him. As soon as John's hold released, Lexie took advantage of the opportunity. "Jackson!" she screamed as loud as she could manage. She gathered more strength in her voice the second time as she called out but it was quickly followed by gunfire, and she feared her cries had gone unheard. John clamped his hand around her mouth and hauled her further into the room before he shoved her against the bed. "Shut the fuck up!"

"Lexie!" her mother gasped from the far corner of the room.

Lexie scrambled off the bed and ran toward her mother. The sight of her immediately brought tears to Lexie's eyes. Her left eye showed the signs of bruising and her lips were swollen. She looked entirely too fragile as Lexie grabbed hold of her to make sure she was real. Her mother wrapped her arms around her and pulled her close. The thin nightgown her mother wore did nothing to hide her weight loss. She looked like a shell of herself, so broken and sad.

"You're all right. You're all right," her mother chanted over and over as she smoothed Lexie's hair.

Lexie pulled back and placed her hands on either side of her mother's face and looked into her tear-filled eyes. "I'm fine, Mom." Lexie gently ran her fingers along the side of her mother's face. "What did he do to you?" Lexie whispered. She felt hot tears run down her cheeks as she took comfort being with her mother again.

"Don't worry about me," her mother said as she pulled Lexie closer again and squeezed tight. They both startled when Jacobs and another man came barreling in the room and Rayner swung the door shut. The man Lexie didn't recognize stumbled into the room and collapsed against the foot of the bed. Lexie's eyes were immediately drawn toward his gun. It had fallen from his hand, landing beside the bed.

Lexie pulled free from her mother and discreetly nudged the gun away with her foot while John,

Jacobs, and Rayner were preoccupied. She tucked it under the bed skirt out of view. She turned back toward her mother, who had also noticed the gun. Her eyes followed Lexie's movements before her eyes flicked up to meet hers.

Lexie turned to look at the man staring blankly at the wall when he made a strange sound. "Are you all right?" Lexie asked when she noticed the color of his skin. He looked up at her and opened his mouth to speak but blood sprayed from his lips. Lexie gasped and covered her mouth as she watched blood pour from his mouth and puddle on his shirt. His head slumped to the side and his eyes slowly glazed over.

Lexie's mother grabbed her hand and pulled away from the man as Jacobs knelt down in front of him and felt for a pulse. He seemed unfazed that the man was dead as he patted him down for weapons and took a few extra clips he had been carrying. He tossed a clip to Rayner. "We'll clear the hall and then we should keep moving toward the exit." Jacobs looked at John for confirmation of the plan. John nodded before he opened the door and Rayner and Jacobs filed out with their guns raised.

The sounds of gunshots filled the hallway and then they heard an explosion. The fire alarm immediately began to sound and its shrill ring cut through the chaos. Lexie instinctively ducked down and covered her ears, unsure of what would follow next. She dropped to the ground to grab for the gun she had tucked away but it was nowhere to be found. She pulled the bed skirt up to reveal a bare floor, panic squeezed her throat tight.

185

Lexie looked up to notice her mother already had the gun in her hands and had it pointed toward John. She shuffled backwards out of the way to see what was happening.

"What do you think you're doing, Mary?" John asked with narrowed eyes.

"What I should have done years ago." Mary held the gun with both hands as she looked over the barrel. Her hands trembled as she held it.

"You can't kill me, Mary, because no matter how much you deny it, you love me," John said. "You can't really live without me and you know it."

"You're wrong," Lexie's mother said, shaking her head like his words were trying to claw their way inside her head. "I hate you."

"Look what you've become." John threw his hand out toward her. "When you were with me you wanted for nothing. Now you live in a small little town and barely have enough money to pay your bills."

"It's you that has nothing, John. I took it all away from you when I left," she gasped as tears fell down her cheeks. "You will never have us."

A loud bang outside the door startled Lexie and it rattled from the impact. She glanced toward the door, sure that someone had knocked it off its hinges. The sound of gunshots filled the room, startling her. Everything seemed surreal as Lexie looked at her mother and then John.

John dropped his gun and grabbed at his stomach. The look of shock painted his features. "You shot me?" He looked up questioningly after he observed his blood-covered fingers pressed against his side.

Lexie stared wide-eyed at John as he swayed on his feet and leaned back against the wall for support. He slowly slid down to the floor and left a smear of blood along the wall with a gasp.

Lexie darted across the room and dropped down in front of John. "Where is Stephanie?" She grabbed his chin and made his eyes meet hers. "I know she isn't home. Tell me," Lexie demanded. "Tell me now!"

"Lexie's little friend looked a lot like the girl with the rose tattoo, didn't she, Mary?" John said with a sinister smile as he glanced over Lexie's shoulder at her mother. "Seemed fitting she meet the same fate, don't ya think?"

"No…" her mother gasped. Lexie spun around to meet her eyes. "I'm so sorry," her mother panted when she looked at Lexie with tears in her eyes.

"Mom?" Lexie watched her as she collapsed against the side of the bed. That's when Lexie noticed her mother's blood saturating the side of her nightgown. The scene had unfolded so quickly she hadn't even realized that John had pulled the trigger as well. "Mom!" Lexie screamed as a heavy dose of fear hit her hard in the chest. She ran toward her as she slipped to the floor. Lexie frenziedly searched for something to press against the wound to stop the blood.

"Stay with me, Mom," Lexie said frantically as she grabbed a pillow from the bed. She ripped the case off it and held it to her mother's side. "Stay with me." Lexie looked up into her face. She could see the pain reflected in her mother's eyes as she struggled to breathe through the pain. Lexie didn't know what to do to save her mother as the she tried to slow her racing mind and figure out a plan. She looked up to where John had fallen to see his body was no longer there. Her heart raced so fast it made her chest hurt.

"We have to get you out of here," Lexie said, picking up her mother's arm and trying to support her weight.

"I can't..." Her mother inhaled sharply when her weight was shifted.

Noise in the hall alerted Lexie that someone was coming. She released her mother's arm and grabbed for the gun on the bed. She wiped her tears with the back of her blood-soaked hand to clear her vision to see the person who entered the room. She couldn't help the thought that this could be the end for them as the gun shook violently in her hand.

"Jackson," Lexie gasped as she dropped back down to the floor. "Help me," she cried. "My mother's been shot."

Jackson lowered his gun after he scanned the room and dropped down next to Lexie. The siren still shrieked loudly around them as Jackson reached for her. As overwhelmed as she was to see him she couldn't look him in the eye. He quickly assessed her mother before he turned toward Lexie and grabbed her shoulder. "We'll get her to the hospital, but I need you to tell me where John is."

"He was just here. Mom shot him, he's injured." Lexie pointed toward the blood on the wall. Dane walked into the room and looked where Lexie was indicating.

"He's not far," Jackson informed him. "He's shot."

Dane nodded before ducking back out of the room and continuing down the hall. Jackson set his gun on the bed and reached for Lexie's mom and pulled her into his arms. "Let's go," Jackson said as he rose to his feet and grabbed his gun while keeping her mother tight to his chest.

Lexie followed close behind with the gun tight in her grasp.

Jackson leaned back through the door to make sure the hallway was clear. "Keep that gun pointed in front of you, Lexie. Shoot at anyone who is not one of us," Jackson ordered.

Lexie shook her head, holding the gun firmly in her hands.

"We need some cover, Ted," Jackson hollered down the hall.

"You got it," Teddy answered, coming into view.

Jackson stepped out into the hall and moved slowly, making sure the rooms were clear as they passed. Dane ducked out of one of the rooms as they approached. "No sign of him." He shook his head, perplexed. "The trail of blood just ends."

"Teddy, get the girls out of here. I have to find him," Jackson said, passing Lexie's mother to Teddy. She was now unconscious and Lexie leaned in close to make sure she was still breathing.

"She'll be okay. Let's go," Teddy said, nodding for Lexie to follow him as they made their way toward the stairwell.

"What about Jackson and Dane?" Lexie asked as she hesitated. She watched Jackson and Dane head in the opposite direction into the now smoke-filled hallway.

"They won't be far behind us. Just don't point that thing at me," Teddy said, looking nervously at the gun in her hand.

Lexie nodded and followed closely on his heels as they made their way toward the stairwell. Teddy moved quickly despite carrying her mother. He stopped at the stairwell door to glance out the small window to make sure no one was behind it. He slowly lowered Lexie's mother to the floor, eliciting a moan from her. "I just need to make sure it's clear," Teddy said. "Hold your gun that way." He pointed back down the hall. "Just don't shoot Jackson or Dane." Teddy disappeared into the stairwell with his gun raised. Lexie stood protectively over her mother, holding her gun up as she looked down the deserted hallway.

Lexie jumped when the door opened again and Teddy resurfaced. "Calm down." Teddy pushed her arm away from him. Lexie didn't even realize she swung the gun around when he opened the door.

"Sorry," she gasped.

Teddy picked up her mother and led them into the stairwell, where they descended a few flights of stairs and came to a lower parking garage. "The police should be arriving any minute if they haven't already, because of the alarm. We need to get out of here undetected and get your mother to the hospital." Teddy kept his voice low. "We can't be seen here." The sound of someone following caught their attention. Teddy held his gun up just as Dane rounded the top of the stairs. "Just me," Dane said,

190

coming down to meet them.

"Where's Jackson?" Lexie asked, watching for him to appear.

"He's still looking for John," Dane said, giving her a reassuring smile.

"Shouldn't you be with him?" Lexie asked nervously.

"He wants you out of here safely. Jackson knows what he's doing, Lexie." Dane pushed the door open and raised his gun before he waved them to follow.

Lexie was in a daze as she was led through the parking garage and into the dark night. The fresh air soothed her senses after spending days inside, but it could not dull the worry that burned in her stomach. She had no answers as to where Stephanie was and the fact that Jackson was still in the building made her sick to her stomach. She tried not to admit to herself that seeing him would bring her overwhelming relief. She tried to convince herself it was only because he was her best chance at finding Stephanie, but the truth was that he was a source of comfort that she craved. Something about him made her feel real and she feared something happening to him.

The sounds of sirens broke through the fire alarm as the emergency vehicles pulled up in front of the building. Lexie could see a crowd gathered in the distance as people were evacuated from the building. "We'll get her to the hospital in time," Dane assured her. He grabbed her by the arm when her pace slowed and pulled her along into the trees. He held onto her as he guided them through the dark wooded area. A few times she tripped, but Dane didn't let her fall. She wasn't sure how they could both see when all she could see was darkness and shadows. So many questions formed on her tongue but she was in too much of a daze to bring herself to speak. She just wanted to get her mother the help she desperately needed.

It wasn't long before they broke from the tree line. Lexie could make out two vehicles parked on the side of the dark street. A man opened the door of the car and began walking toward them when he noticed them arrive.

"Stay here and wait for Jackson," Teddy said to him as he rounded the van. Teddy stopped in front of the back doors of the cargo van. Dane released Lexie and swung the doors open so Teddy could set her mother down.

"We're going to St. Lux hospital," Dane said as he walked around the van and opened the driver's door. Lexie grabbed Teddy's hand after he climbed in the back and he pulled her up.

"Let's go."

CHAPTER
TWENTY-ONE

Jackson

The buzz of the fluorescent light overhead in the hospital waiting room slowly grated on Jackson's nerves. He was already coiled tight with emotions and he was trying to keep himself under control.

He sat across from Lexie in the uncomfortable grey chairs that made up the seating area. She had been staring at an envelope in her hands for the last hour, seemingly memorizing every detail of the paper. She had washed the blood from her hands but she still had some staining the front of her dress. Every once in a while he would catch her looking down at it, as if reminding herself what had happened.

Jackson wanted to ask her what was in the envelope that had her so captivated but she hadn't spoken a word since he arrived. He wanted to know what she was thinking about as she sat in front of him, looking so fragile and exhausted. Ideas of what happened to her while she was held captive kept running through his head. He wanted to know if there was anyone else he needed to add to his kill list. He would kill every last one of Stodden's men if he had to.

All Jackson could see was her and she insisted on looking everywhere but at him. She was avoiding him and he didn't want to intrude on her thoughts. It was best to keep his distance for now because he knew she was angry with him but he didn't expect it to pain him so much.

Jackson had been beside himself with worry for her safety since she was taken and now that she was here with him, he had an overwhelming desire to wrap his arms around her and hold her close. Her body language toward him kept him in his seat. He didn't want to cause her any more distress than he already had. He knew he had to wait for her to make the first move.

Jackson leaned forward, resting his elbows on his knees, and raked his hands through his hair. He was angry that had been so close he could even remember the lingering scent of Stodden's cologne in the halls as he searched room by room. Unfortunately, Stodden had provisions in place to escape. Jackson had searched every square foot before he admitted defeat and he had to accept Stodden had slipped through his fingers.

The firemen had started to infiltrate the floors that Stodden's men had used when he slipped out. It was only a matter of time before they found the bodies. Jackson knew he couldn't be anywhere near the mess when it was revealed. Everything depended on him keeping a low profile.

Lexie's mother was in surgery and they were waiting quietly for news from the doctor. She had lost a lot of blood and was in critical condition when she arrived. Jackson looked up and noticed Teddy watching him. He gave Jackson a sad smile before he walked toward Lexie and sat down beside her.

"How are you holding up?" Teddy asked as he nudged her gently with his shoulder.

Lexie looked up at him from under her thick, damp lashes and shrugged in response. "Where's Evan?" she asked quietly. "I need him." Her words stung more than Jackson cared to admit.

Teddy's gaze shot toward Jackson. "Ha, funny story," Teddy said, rubbing the back of his neck with an awkward laugh. "He's actually at a strip club."

"What?" Lexie's scowl shadowed her entire face and Teddy's face fell. "Now?" She shook her head, trying to make sense of Teddy's explanation. "Does he know Stephanie's still missing?"

"Well, as you know, things aren't always straight forward..." Teddy began.

"Just spill it," Lexie said severely, like she knew the hole they were in was about to get deeper.

Teddy looked around the room, making sure no one outside their group was in hearing distance. "He's sort of collateral. John has lots of enemies, and we had to play nice to ensure we had what we needed to eliminate him," Teddy said uneasily. "While you were away, things got a little complicated." He looked nervous sitting beside Lexie trying to explain details he knew would upset her.

"But you didn't eliminate John," Lexie said cautiously. "So what does that mean for Evan?"

"It doesn't mean anything," Jackson spoke up. "He won't get hurt. I promise." Lexie still didn't look at him as he silently begged her to.

"Right now we need to focus on making sure your mother is all right." Teddy patted her uncomfortably on the knee before he looked over at Jackson. "Evan is most definitely having a better time than we are."

"We need to find Stephanie," Lexie said, looking up at Jackson for the first time since he arrived and he was hit with the full impact of her intense gaze.

"She wasn't there. I looked everywhere, Lex," he responded dejectedly. The pain she was in was written all over her beautiful features.

"Jacks," Dane called to him from across the waiting room.

Jackson looked up to see Giles heading their way. "Shit," Jackson muttered under his breath. He knew it was only a matter of time before Giles found them. Jackson stood up and watched him approach with a fierce scowl upon his face.

Giles pointed at Teddy and Dane. "Don't go anywhere because I want to have a chat with the both of you as well."

Jackson followed Giles as he led him around the corner to an empty hallway with a run of vending machines. Giles looked at Jackson before he reached in his pocket and grabbed some change. He walked over to one of the machines and started shoving coins into the coffee dispenser. He grabbed the bridge of his nose and took a deep breath as he watched the cup fill with thick, syrupy fluid.

Giles picked up the cup and tipped it to his lips. The coffee was barely in his mouth before he spit it back into the cup and tossed it into the nearest garbage bin. He spun around to face Jackson. "Please tell me there is a logically, un-incriminating reason that you end up in a hospital hours after an attack on a hotel that is now being investigated as a hideout for John Stodden." Giles raked his hand through his grey hair. "Oh, and let's not forget the fact that you are here with Mary Connors and her daughter, who had been, until now, known to be in his possession." Giles stopped speaking and waited as a nurse passed them by and was a safe distance away. "Please tell me you didn't try to take John down by yourself when he was basically in an armed fortress surrounded by civilians?"

"Okay, I won't," Jackson responded, knowing it was impossible to deny.

"Jesus," Giles said in disbelief, knowing full well Jackson was lying. He raked his hand down his face and adjusted the collar of his shirt. "What were you thinking? I can't keep covering for you." Giles waved his hands to dramatize his point. "This is beyond, Jackson. I mean, where the hell did you get the guns? I know you're smart enough not to go in there with police issued weapons. Actually, don't tell me. I don't want to fucking know." He held his hand up to stop Jackson from answering. Anger rolled off his shoulders in waves. "I'm the fucking police commissioner." Giles hit himself in the chest.

"I never asked you to cover for me," Jackson said when Giles' rant died off and he was left looking at Jackson for answers.

"That's what family does," Giles said sadly.

"You aren't my family, Giles. My family is dead. They're all fucking dead." Jackson squared his jaw. He was too fueled with emotion for this conversation. He was bound to combust from the strain.

"You have never been more wrong, Jackson. Who do you think those guys are out there who risked their necks and their jobs for you?"

"Dane and Teddy didn't have anything to do with it. I'm the one who did this."

Giles tilted his head in disbelief.

"Take my badge but you need them."

"I need you too!" Giles hollered before correcting his tone. "You three are the best fucking cops I have, but you keep insisting on fucking everything up. The only thing going for you is that you get results." Giles shook his head. "At least you had the sense to go to a hospital far enough away from the hotel that it will not be connected and admitted Mary as a Jane Doe. I can work with that and tidy things up so this does not explode in your face," Giles said as if he was trying to assure himself as much as Jackson.

"How did you find us, anyway?" Jackson asked.

"You don't think I know you well enough to have connections in every hospital in the state?"

Jackson bit his lip and shook his head thoughtfully. "I almost had him, Giles."

"I have told you so many times. You're too close to this. You don't think clearly." Giles grabbed Jackson's shoulder.

Jackson shook his head. "I will do this." Jackson looked into Giles' concern filled eyes. He would not budge on this. He would make sure Giles knew that this was something he needed to see through.

Giles sighed and let his hand fall. "I can maybe buy you a couple of weeks if I put you three on an undercover case, but I can't help you. It won't take long for Haffey to realize someone is making waves in her pool and you'll be the first person she'll come after. That woman is like a shark. As soon as anyone gets word of what you're doing, it's over. I'll take care of the paperwork here to cover your tracks at the hospital so Haffey or anyone else doesn't get wind of Mary's admittance here. I handled the local authorities when I arrived. As soon as they realized they had a gunshot victim, flags were raised. I think I curbed it before it had a chance to leak. What would you have done if I hadn't shown up to stop an investigation?"

"I always think of something." Jackson smiled with a raised brow.

Giles shook his head with a smile. "You are so much like your father."

Giles' words hit him in the chest and he felt like they stole his breath. "Thanks, Giles," Jackson said, knowing how much of a risk Giles was taking with him.

"Don't thank me yet." Giles started to walk away. "Two weeks, tops," he warned.

"Giles?" Jackson called after him. Giles swung

around to face him. "Don't trust anyone."

Giles narrowed his eyes. "Do you know who the rat is?" Giles asked.

Jackson nodded his head. "I believe so but I need proof first."

"Who is it?"

"I don't know for certain." Jackson was wary to admit it. He still had a hard time believing the truth himself.

Tell me who it is, Jackson," Giles demanded.

Jackson squeezed his eyes shut before he let the word pass his lips. "Rosh." Jackson opened his eyes to see his reaction.

"Fuck," Giles said, shaking his head. "You better get some proof. You can't accuse someone like Rosh without having a solid case. Things just went from bad to fucked."

"To be honest, when I saw you storming in here, I thought you were gonna take my badge and throw me in a cell," Jackson admitted.

"Would it really make a difference? You would find a way regardless." Giles looked Jackson in the eye. "I'll do the best I can to keep this under wraps, but I fear you may have dug a hole too deep this time," Giles said.

"You can't really be surprised?" Jackson asked as he tried to lighten the mood.

"Stay alive, Jackson, because *you* are *my* family." Giles patted Jackson on the shoulder before heading back toward Dane and Teddy.

Jackson stared after him. He knew he should be sitting in a cell right now for what he had done. For some reason Giles believed in him and he needed to make sure he didn't let him down.

Jackson walked toward Lexie, who was still sitting in the same chair she'd been in since he arrived. This time he sat down next to her. He tried to ignore the delight that rushed to the surface of his dark sea of emotions when his arm brushed against hers. Something about her was like a warm sun to his senses and it was impossible to deny her effect on him.

He scrambled desperately for something right to say to her but all his thoughts came to a complete stop when she spoke first.

"I think I know where Stephanie is," Lexie said, looking up at him with a sudden bright flame behind her eyes. "I asked John where she was and he told me she would suffer the same fate as the girl from my mother's diary, the girl with the rose tattoo who went missing years ago. My mother told me it was the man with the scar that took her." Lexie pointed toward the side of her neck. "I saw him when I was there. His name is Terrance Masten."

"The mayor of Belhaven?"

Lexie nodded her head. "He has Stephanie. I'm sure of it."

Jackson collapsed back into his chair and rubbed his jaw.

"He had an expensive suit on with a red tie. I can still remember that jagged scar down the side of his neck."

"That's definitely him," Jackson said, leaning his head back and staring at the ceiling.

He could feel Lexie's eyes on him and he wished more than anything all the noise between them could just go away but the truth was too loud to ignore. "It's not gonna be easy to get close to him."

"But we have to," Lexie said as she grabbed onto his forearm. "We have to."

"I know."

She pulled her hand away quickly when Jackson looked down at it.

"Dane will stay here with you and wait for your mother to get out of surgery. Teddy and I will start digging. If Masten has her, then we will find out."

Lexie nodded and quickly wiped away a tear that escaped her eyes. Jackson stood up and motioned at Teddy across the room as he and Teddy resurfaced.

"Jackson…" Lexie called out to him as he started to walk away. He looked back at her, glimpsing the torment behind her gaze. She looked as if she was struggling to find the words.

"As soon as we find out anything I will let you know," Jackson assured her.

CHAPTER TWENTY-TWO

Jackson

The hotel room smelled musty with a lingering scent of chemical pine. Jackson dropped his keys on the small desk by the window and flicked on the lights. The room looked as if it had its original décor and was in dire need of a facelift, though Jackson didn't give it much more thought as it would serve its purpose well enough. He would have preferred his apartment but he couldn't afford the time and he didn't want to be far from Lexie. Jackson looked around the room, opening drawers and looking behind curtains. He had lived this life long enough to know not to assume anything.

Jackson headed toward the bathroom and turned on the light. The bathroom was as appealing as the rest of the room but at least it smelled as if it was recently cleaned. He pulled back the curtain to reveal a rust-stained tub but the curtain seemed relatively new. Once he was satisfied that nothing seemed out of the ordinary, he hit the switch on the wall and walked back out into the main area.

Teddy walked into the room with his bag slung over his shoulder. "Wow, this place looks exactly like the backdrop for a porn I saw years ago."

"You actually paid attention to the background?" Jackson asked in disbelief.

"Well, I did watch it a lot." Teddy unzipped his bag and pulled out his laptop and set it on the desk. "Just in case it is the same place, don't touch the walls." Teddy laughed. "Or wear bare feet on the carpet."

Jackson looked down at the brown shag carpet under his boots and cringed. "I'll keep my boots on. I won't take any chances. What about the bed?"

"You're safe there," Teddy reassured.

"You get off on some crazy shit, Teddy." Jackson shook his head before he laid back on the bed and kicked his feet up.

Teddy shrugged dismissively as he turned on his computer and sat down. He rubbed his hands together before cracking his knuckles. "Let's see what Masten is hiding other than his father's dirty little secret."

Jackson tucked his hands behind his head and leaned back on the pillow. "Giles rip a strip off you?" Jackson asked as he stared up at the ceiling.

"What do you think?" Teddy looked back over his shoulder. "We got off easier than I expected, though. I was right that he wants us to stay on task even though he can't admit it. He wants Stodden as much as we do but he has no jurisdiction. He's taking as much of a risk as we are."

"Yeah, I know," Jackson said thoughtfully. He thought about what Giles had said about him being his family. When it came to verbalizing feelings, neither one of them were very successful, so his confession surprised Jackson. Giles was a man who had devoted his life to his job and her personal life suffered for it. Jackson had fallen onto his plate as a troubled young man with no direction. Jackson knew Giles did his best when it came to providing a stable environment for him. They were both such strong minded people but somewhere along the way they had grown to understand each other. Jackson never realized that Giles considered him family. He believed he was just a liability because he felt obligated toward Jackson's father, who had been one of his closest friends before his death.

If Jackson was honest with himself, he had to admit that Giles had filled the shoes of that role better than anyone could have, considering Jackson's state of mind. He was a lost soul with no hope of a future. Giles reminded him he had a purpose and he chose that to be avenging his father. That very thing is what he focused on as he began the journey of turning his life around. He began to walk a straight line so that one day he could destroy everything that caused the demise of his father.

Jackson pulled out his phone and looked up the picture of Lexie. He had lost count of how many times he had looked to it for comfort. Lexie was a warm inviting light in his cold, dark life and she began to illuminate elements of his life he had taken for granted or overlooked when he was living with his blinders on. She was the reason he wished there was more for him in this life.

She had looked so fragile curled up in the chair beside Dane when he left hospital. He hated leaving her but he knew he was better off with Teddy looking for Stephanie. That is what Lexie wanted from him right now and he didn't want to disappoint her any more than he already had. Being close to her made his head swim with thoughts he knew he shouldn't indulge in.

Jackson sat up cautiously when he noticed a shadow slowly pass the curtained window and linger just outside the door. Jackson swung his legs off the bed and grabbed for his gun from the nightstand. He placed his finger against his lips when Teddy looked at him and motioned toward the window. Teddy picked up his gun and stood up from his chair.

Jackson crouched down and walked toward the door as Teddy readied his gun. He glanced through the peephole. A figure hovered just out of sight until they stepped forward and Jackson could identify him. He lowered his gun with a shake of his head and unlocked the door. He swung the door open and grabbed Nate by the shirt and hauled him in the room.

"What the fuck are you doing sneaking up on us? You know better than that," Jackson growled angrily as he pulled him inside.

"I had nowhere else to go," Nate said as he walked in the room. He turned around to face Jackson with a defeated look. "How's the woman? Did she make it?"

"Yeah," Jackson said as he placed his gun back on the nightstand. "She was still in surgery when we left."

Nate nodded his head. "Good, 'cause she didn't look so good when I saw her." Nate scratched the back of his neck. "So what about the other girl?"

"What about her?" Jackson said a little harsher than he intended.

Nate raised his hands "Okay, okay, I get it." He dropped his weight on the bed. "So what are the two of you up to hiding away in this hotel?"

"We were trying to get away from you," Teddy said with a teasing smile.

"Isn't everyone?" Nate responded lightly.

"Why are you hanging around, Nate?" Jackson asked seriously.

"I still want to help. I owe you for saving my ass plenty of times back then," Nate admitted a bit uncomfortably.

"We were fucking kids, Nate. I already told you, you don't owe me anything. Seth is gone. This is the chance for you to make a clean break from this."

"And do what, Jacks? Get a job? Get married? I don't know how to live a normal life. This fucked up version of the world that I have is all I know."

"You okay with this, Ted?" Jackson asked when he noticed Teddy watching them.

"Picking up strays seems to be our new thing." He smiled before he started typing on his computer again.

Jackson heard voices outside and walked toward the door to peer out again. He watched a couple walk by and head toward another room, seemingly in a hurry for privacy.

"You still as paranoid as ever?" Nate said when Jackson faced him.

"It's the reason I'm still alive. How did you make it all these years?" Jackson asked.

"A bloody, fucking miracle," Nate said. "Apparently someone still wants me alive." Nate waved to the ceiling.

Jackson looked up with raised brows. "Don't tell me you believe in God now?"

Nate shrugged his shoulders. "Nah, my mother did, and look where that got her. It's more of a just in case thing."

"So tell me, have you been living under Seth's wing all these years?" Jackson asked curiously.

"Yeah, Black kicked me to the curb first chance he got because I reminded him of you. He was pretty foul about your untimely exit for a long time. I hooked up with Seth's crew to keep myself alive because I'm a sucker for punishment."

"Aren't we all?" Jackson agreed.

"It seems you're getting yourself into more than your fair share of trouble these days," Nate said devilishly. "Some things never change."

"No, they certainly don't." Jackson dropped down in an armchair in the corner of the room. "Listen, Nate, I keep my circle tight because I don't trust easily. If I suspect that you're anything but truthful, I won't hesitate," Jackson warned, knowing Nate would understand exactly what he meant.

Nate stayed quiet for a moment, watching Jackson before he nodded his head. "Yeah, I get that."

Jackson pushed off the chair and walked toward the mini fridge in the corner of the room. He grabbed three minis of rum and tossed one toward Nate, who caught it effortlessly. Jackson walked toward Teddy and sat his down next to his computer. "Look for anything you can find about a lake house," Jackson said, watching the screen. Teddy had multiple windows of information littering the monitor. The speed in which he navigated through files always mystified Jackson. Jackson cracked the top of the bottle and tipped it up to his lips. The cheap rum burned his throat and tasted less than desirable but it did the trick.

"At first glance, this fuck is cleaner than a nun in confession," Teddy said as he skimmed multiple files.

"We know he likes to hide things. Seth was a testament to that." Jackson placed his hand on Teddy's shoulder. "I'm gonna leave you to sift through whatever the hell you're doing." Jackson waved toward his screen. "Nate, you're with me. We need to go visit Black."

Nate's color turned a little grey. "That man hates me, Jackson." He shook his head and sat up from his reclined position on the bed.

"Black hates everyone. We just have to make sure we are not at the top of the list," Jackson said with a smirk.

"Are you?" Nate asked as he rose to his feet.

"That's what we are going to find out." Jackson holstered his gun and slipped his phone into his pocket. "Call me if you find anything," he said to

Teddy.

"Yep," Teddy replied without taking his eyes off the screen.

Jackson caught Nate when he made the sign of the cross and glared at him. "What? It can't hurt," Nate said defensively.

Jackson shook his head with a sigh before he headed toward the door.

CHAPTER TWENTY-THREE

Stephanie

The sound of silence was deafening as Stephanie paced the cell back and forth. It felt heavy and solid as it surrounded her. Initially she had started counting every step she took, trying to distract her mind, but the numbers became so high that they took too long to say and she grew too tired to think. She was parched and her tongue felt too large for her mouth. It was the longest stretch of time since he had come. She desperately needed water and her stomach ached with hunger. She wished she could have some indication of when it was day and night so she didn't feel so disoriented.

She didn't understand why he was punishing her this time. Scenarios kept running through her head about why he had not returned. She wondered if something had happened to him or if he grew tired of her and she would be left to starve. The thought of slowly wasting away made her stomach clench painfully.

Stephanie began to hum the tune that had been stuck in her head. It brought her some comfort and made her feel less scared in the darkness. The feel of the metal bars had become familiar to her hands as she wrapped her fingers around them. She leaned her head against the cool metal and found it offered some relief to her growing headache.

Stephanie hadn't been able to stop thinking about Rose, the girl who he apparently believed her to be. She wondered if she had died within these bars as she believed she soon would. Her initial hope of someone finding her had slowly faded away to be left with acceptance that her time was drawing to an end. She stopped thinking about the people she loved because it became too painful.

The sound of her voice echoed in the room, making her feel less alone. Every once in a while she would stop humming when she believed she could hear someone else singing along but it was only her imagination. The desolation had a way of toying with her sanity.

Stephanie walked toward the small cot, the only thing that offered the slightest amount of comfort from the damp cold. She grabbed the thin sheet and wrapped it around herself before sitting back against the wall.

Stephanie jumped when something thumped against the door on the far side of the room. The door rattled on its hinges with a resounding thud. She held the blanket tighter as she held her breath. Her heart beat pulsed in her ears so loud she couldn't hear anything else. She was unsure what would come of his return. He was normally so quiet when he unlatched the door but this time was different.

Fear rushed potently in her blood, a familiar feeling that had its claws dug deep within her. The promise of death loomed over her like a heavy fog she could no longer see past. She could no longer recognize herself anymore. She was cast into a darkness that was slowly eating her alive and what remained was forever changed. This man robbed her of the person she was and she didn't know how to get used to what was left.

Even though she had searched endlessly many times before, she dropped to the floor and desperately searched for something sharp like a stone or a piece of concrete—anything that could possibly be used for protection. She flipped the bed on its side and ran her fingers along the coarse material for springs she could pry free but there was nothing. She had no way to defend herself against the man she knew any second would walk through the door.

Finally the door swung open. Stephanie froze, watching his looming shadow in the doorway. At first he didn't move and she thought she was imagining him. That hope collapsed when he took a step into the room and the dim light cast strange shadows on his features. Normally he was eerily composed but now he seemed rattled. His hair was in disarray and his tie was missing. His shirt was untucked and most of the buttons undone like he had frantically pulled at his clothes. Stephanie backed against the far wall, scared of what this version of him meant for her.

"My Rose...my sweet, sweet Rose," he whispered in a tone that made all the hairs stand up on her skin.

Stephanie didn't move as she pressed herself harder into the wall and prayed he did not enter her cell. She immediately began to think this could be the end and it terrified her. As much as she had suffered by his hands she still wanted to live. She wanted to be able to see the people she loved again and feel the sun upon her skin.

"He's dead," his voice cracked with his confession. Lexie held her breath as his words hit her. She had no idea who he was talking about, but it did nothing to lessen the fear of what it could mean.

"My father always loved him more than me. No matter what I did, it was always him, him...*him.*" He began to run his fingers along the bars, the rough iron material making harsh rubbing sounds against his skin. He seemed a bit lost in his thoughts as he spoke. "His dying words to me after a lifetime of trying to make him notice me were to protect *him*. I did everything for my father and still he beat me. He beat me so hard I couldn't move for days."

He stopped rubbing the bars and looked up at Stephanie. "Despite everything, I did what he asked. I always looked out for him but now he's dead. I didn't do the only thing my father asked of me. I didn't do the one thing," his words turned angry as he listened to himself speak. "I didn't protect his other son...Seth." He grabbed the bars with both hands. "You know, I always hated that name. My mother hated him too, but she hated us all. She told me I reminded her too much of my father. It always confused me why Father couldn't see I was a better son, so I tried harder to make him see."

Stephanie was surprised by his confession. He never once mentioned anything about his personal life. He had always been so closed off and terrifyingly inhuman. It wasn't until he stumbled away from the bars and dropped himself to the ground that she realized he was drunk.

"I had gone to see her...the woman my father preferred over my mother. I thought she would be some faceless woman but she wasn't...she was just a girl," his words broke off in a sob. "She had been in my class at school until she left to have a baby. No one knew who the father was. She had only been fourteen—my age. Her parents said nothing because my father paid them off. They kept his secret and let him continue to see her." He shuffled closer to the bars and leaned against them.

"Clara was her name. She was actually my first guest here, although it wasn't until much later after I acquired this property. She wasn't young anymore then."

Stephanie felt sick to her stomach with his confession.

"I wanted to know why my father loved her so much. I fucked her over and over, trying to feel what he felt for her, but she wouldn't stop screaming. I had to make her stop because she wouldn't stop." He hit the bars angrily.

"Years later, I asked him why he had loved Clara

so much. Do you know what he said?" He looked at Stephanie expectantly.

Stephanie managed a small shake of her head.

"Because she was weak and pliable, but I discovered that she was not at all what he thought she was. She fought more than any of the others. She scratched and clawed until the very end when I wrapped my hands around her neck and squeezed." He grabbed the bars and twisted his hands. "But that was before I found you, Rose. Before I found out you were *my* Clara."

"My father was never the same after he lost her and I felt the same way after I lost you too, but then I started seeing parts of you in others, so I would bring them here; the same hair, the same skin tone, the same elegant fingers. Though none of them were you, I could see it in their eyes. I didn't think I would ever find you again, no matter how hard I tried, and how many I brought here."

Stephanie wanted to ask him how many girls he had locked in these very walls but she was too terrified to know the truth. The way he had said "others" chilled her to the bone. When he discovered she was not his Rose she would become one of them and suffer the same fate. The only thing she knew with all certainty was that she was not the first to shed tears behind these bars.

"You won't leave me again, will you, Rose?" He leaned his head against the bar and started to mumble a sound. At first she didn't recognize the tune that slurred from his lips. Then the words started to formulate the song that had played in her head since she had woken that first day as a prisoner. It was his song that had been stuck in her head. The realization made her stomach feel like lead. She would never utter it again.

His words died off and he turned to her. "Sing for me, Rose," he asked.

Stephanie shook her head. "I'm too tired," Stephanie said with a raw voice. "Thirsty." She slid to the floor and grabbed her knees. She knew she couldn't bring herself to sing that song.

"You are my Rose, right? I finally found you again?" He pressed his face between the bars.

Stephanie nodded her head and pushed a strangled "yes" between her lips. She was too frightened to discover what would happen if she didn't agree. She could still feel his hand against her neck and knew how easy it would be for him to kill her if he chose.

"Good…good. Are you hungry?" He turned and began stumbling toward the door. "I will get you some food. Maybe something sweet." He spun back around and threw her a smile. "Yeah, something sweet for my Rose."

Stephanie didn't release her breath until he disappeared through the door. As hungry as she was, she wished he would never return.

CHAPTER TWENTY-FOUR

Jackson

"I swore I'd never come back to this place," Nate said as they parked on the side of the street and looked up at the sign of Black's strip club, Shimmy Shakers. As far as strip joints went, this one had some class. The exterior was well maintained and discreet, only showcasing silhouettes of female figures with discreet black on black applications. Tall, dim bar lights framed in the large awning that offered privacy to customers who entered the premises.

"The last time I saw Slash he threatened to cut my balls off. I'm rather attached to them. Maybe I should wait in the car," Nate suggested.

"Slash threatens to cut everyone's balls off. He said the same thing to me last time I saw him. Let's go." Jackson opened his door and stepped out onto the sidewalk. If he was honest with himself, he wasn't looking forward to this meeting, either, though it wasn't Slash he was concerned about. He was just a bully with a blade and Jackson could handle him.

Black had the upper hand on Jackson when it came to their current predicament and it was not a situation he liked to be in. He needed to buy more time to keep Evan alive. He knew Black would not hesitate to kill Evan. He needed to convince Black that it was in his best interest not to. Jackson still had every intention to kill Stodden. In fact, he was more fueled than ever knowing Stodden was injured and his numbers were down.

Ideally, he would still be on his trail day and night until he found the hole where Stodden was lying low. It was the perfect time to strike but Stephanie and Evan were factors he was not used to dealing with. This was the reason why he lived his life without connections to people that would prove to be a liability, but he needed to make sure both were safe. He knew Lexie would not forgive him otherwise. He wanted to piece her life back together as much as possible with a desire that drove him more than anything else.

The music poured from the interior as Jackson pulled open the front door. Two intimidating bouncers stood on either side of the interior entrance to instill fear into anyone thinking about stepping out of line. Jackson brushed past them without a second thought. He was intent on seeking out Black as quickly as possible. They didn't have the luxury of time. Black would have caught wind of the fact that Stodden was still alive by now.

Nate fell in step behind Jackson as he kept his eyes out for Black. Jackson noticed a familiar face from Black's crew heading in their direction with two women hanging off his arms. Jackson flagged him down and asked him where to find Black. The man pointed offhandedly toward a roped off section toward the back of the bar before he carried on with his company.

When Jackson approached, a bouncer stepped in his way, letting him know it was off limits. "No entry," the man said as he crossed his arms over his skin tight black t-shirt. The man's head was shaved and he wore a goatee. He looked every bit the stereotypical bouncer.

"I'm here to see Black," Jackson said irritably.

"He's not seeing anyone tonight," he replied, refusing to allow Jackson to pass.

"He'll see me," Jackson insisted as he looked over the man's shoulder and noted that Black had already learned of his arrival. Black stood up from his current company and waved toward the bouncer to allow Jackson to enter. The man stood back and unlatched the rope as he practically growled at the two of them.

"Nice shirt. Does it come in men's too?" Jackson smirked as he passed.

"Are you trying to get yourself killed?" Nate asked in disbelief as he looked back at the bouncer, who was barely containing himself. "I'm pretty sure that guy has serious 'roid rage issues."

"You worry too much, Nate." Jackson shook his head.

"Someone has to, you never have."

Jackson dismissed Nate as he approached Black, who did not look amused. A scowl carved deep into his brow. Nate grew quiet as Black's eyes fell on him and then looked back at Jackson with a raised brow. "Follow me," Black said.

Jackson glanced at Nate, who seemed a little unsure about the situation, but surprisingly determined to stay by his side. Nate had changed over the last decade and it made guilt settle in his stomach. He should have fought harder for his old friend, but back then he could see nothing through his own hatred.

The past was now water under the bridge and Nate was once again his wingman. This time he felt as if he would be able to depend on him when the waves started crashing. Jackson had always seen a part of himself in Nate. It was one of the many reasons they'd created an unconventional bond all those years ago when Jackson refused to let anyone else close.

Black led them away from the group he had been entertaining toward a booth. He waved toward a waitress as he sat down. The waitress immediately approached their table with a friendly smile on her face. "What can I get you gentlemen?" She placed her hand on her hip and cast them a flirtatious smile.

"Whiskey on the rocks," Jackson answered without pause.

"I'll have a draft," Nate followed.

Black gave the waitress a nod before she spun on her heels and sauntered away.

"So I assume you are here to enlighten me as to

why Stodden is still alive?" Black grabbed the edge of the table, throwing a displeased expression toward Jackson.

"He is for now, but that will soon change. He's injured and licking his wounds," Jackson said confidently.

"That's not what we agreed." Black leaned back in his seat. "Tell me why I shouldn't put a bullet in my little house guest?" He waved toward the back of the bar, where Jackson knew the offices and private rooms were located...the very place he assumed they were keeping Evan.

"It's as good as done. I just need more time. You know Stodden as well as anyone. You know how resourceful the fucker can be," Jackson defended his case.

"Your guy fucked one of my girls," Black said before clenching his jaw.

"No offence, Black, but some of your girls have fucked their way through this entire bar." Jackson didn't even try to stay on safe ground as he addressed Black. "Don't let the fact that one of your girls popped his cherry to cloud the bigger picture. Evan is harmless, but I need him after this is all said and done. I will get to Stodden and finish this, you have my word."

The waitress returned with three glasses on her tray, smilingly wildly despite the tension between the men she was serving. "There you go," she said warmly before darting off to her next customer.

Black tipped his glass up to his lips and took a sip before setting the glass down on the table and gazing calculatedly at Jackson. "I'll give you a week."

"What's the catch?" Jackson narrowed his eyes.

"You work for me after you kill Stodden and I will let your friend live," Black said as his lips curled up in a sinister smile. He was enjoying having Jackson backed into a corner. Jackson knew this had been his plan all along.

"And if I refuse?" Jackson asked.

"Then I will kill him and you," Black threatened.

"Clear enough," Jackson said. He picked up his glass and tossed the whiskey down his throat, relishing in the blissful burn of the liquor.

"I see the two of you are together again," Black raised his brow. "Did Nate mention that his sticky fingers have gotten him into trouble? Now that Seth is out of the picture I would imagine they'll come to collect what he owes."

"I'll deal with Nate," Jackson said defensively, knowing Black was trying to rattle him.

"Very well," Black said, taking another drink.

"We'll need to see Evan before we leave," Jackson insisted.

Black waved toward one of his men standing off to the side.

"A word of advice, Jackson," Black said, running his finger around the lip of his glass. "The fastest way to a man's downfall is the love of a woman."

Jackson narrowed his eyes in confusion. "Why the fuck are you telling me this?"

"You have the look of a man under the foot of a woman." Black laughed at Jackson's discomfort. "I know about the girl. I wouldn't be a good business man if I didn't look into all the details."

"The girl has nothing to do with this or me," Jackson countered, keeping his emotions in check.

"Of course she doesn't," Black said sarcastically.

The bouncer approached the table. "Take them to see our guest before they leave," Black ordered. Jackson slid out of the booth to follow the man.

"Jackson?" Black called after him. "If you don't kill Stodden, I will kill everyone you hold dear, starting with that girl."

"Stodden is already dead. I just have to deliver the message," Jackson replied before turning his back on Black before he did something he would regret. His fists were clenched so tight he thought his nails might have broken skin.

The man led the down a long corridor until they came to an open door, and then waved them inside. Jackson took one step inside the spacious room and his eyes landed on Evan handcuffed to a barred window. He was lying unconscious against a woman sitting next to him on the sofa, though on further inspection, Jackson noted there were subtle features that gave her secret away. Jackson assumed she could no longer be considered a male from what he could see. In fact, she was strikingly beautiful for someone not born a female.

"Well, hello, Duke. You come to collect Country?" she asked, looking him over.

"More like check to make sure he's still alive," Jackson answered as he kicked Evan's foot but got no response. "Wake up, Evan. This isn't a fucking party."

"You certainly don't have a soft touch, do you?"

she asked with a raised brow.

"Not for him," Jackson answered truthfully. "What'd he take?"

"Not sure. One of the girls sunk her claws into him and left before I could question her." She tapped Evan on the cheek. "Country, wake up. Wake up."

Evan turned his face into her shoulder and raised his free hand up, landing on the woman's breast. He fondled her for a moment before he became fully awake and opened his eyes. He looked up to see whose he was groping. "Cherry?" Evan pulled back. "Did we make out?" Evan asked groggily.

"*We* didn't do anything, darling, but *you* did feel me up quite a bit on more than one occasion."

"Shit, sorry." Evan moved to sit up but the quick movements caused his color to noticeably whiten. "I'm gonna be sick."

Nate grabbed a garbage can and passed it to Evan just in time. His cuffs rattled against the bars and his skin was noticeably raw. When Evan was finished emptying his stomach, he looked up with one eye open. "Aren't you the guy from the farm house?" Evan asked before spitting in the bucket.

"Yeah." Nate shrugged.

"The girls?" Evan said in a rush as he looked up at Jackson. "What happened?"

"Lexie is safe and her mother is in the hospital. John shot her, but according to the doctors, they were very hopeful she would make a full recovery."

Evan ran his hand down over his face. "Stephanie?"

"Still working on finding her, but we have a

225

good lead," Jackson informed him.

"Good. Get me the fuck out of here so I can get to the hospital." Evan rattled his cuff.

"There is one more thing," Jackson added.

Evan's eyes snapped up to Jackson's face. "What?" he asked bluntly, as if knowing it would be bad news for him.

"We didn't exactly kill Stodden yet, so you get an extended stay," Jackson said unapologetically.

Evan sighed and leaned back against the sofa. "I can't stay here. I need to see Lexie," he complained.

"You will after we take care of him. Black already promised not to kill you, so just relax."

Evan threw Jackson a dirty look. "I really do hate you," he confessed.

"The feeling is mutual," Jackson replied. He retrieved his wallet and pulled out some bills. "Do you mind making sure he doesn't OD before I can get him out of here? I need this idiot alive."

"I'll try," Cherry said, taking the money.

"We have to go," Jackson said to Evan just as he grabbed for the garbage can again. Evan began to protest but his stomach wouldn't comply.

Nate didn't say a word until they slipped back into Jackson's car. "You're not really going to work for Black, are you?"

"Not a chance," Jackson replied confidently.

"So what are you going to do?"

"One problem at a time, Nate. First we find Stephanie before it's too late, if we aren't already."

CHAPTER TWENTY-FIVE

Lexie

"Lexie?" the nurse called out as she entered the waiting room.

Lexie practically jumped out of her seat and looked expectantly at the nurse. Dane, who had been asleep in a chair across from her, jolted awake.

"You can see your mother now." The nurse smiled as she watched Dane collect himself from the abrupt wake up.

"Thank you so much," Lexie blurted happily. She turned around to see if Dane was going to join her.

"I'll wait here." He yawned.

Lexie followed the nurse down the hall into her mother's room. "She's still groggy from the medication, but she should come around soon," the nurse said as she laid a gentle hand on Lexie's shoulder. She reminded Lexie of the librarian from home. She was always so kind and motherly to everyone. "Push the button by her bed if you need anything."

Lexie nodded as she left the room. A sob escaped Lexie's lips as she looked at her mother in the hospital bed. She immediately grabbed her mother's hand and covered it with her own. "I was so scared, Mom," Lexie admitted softly. She sat on the edge of the bed and watched the gentle rising and falling of her mother's chest. Her mother responded with a gentle squeeze of her hand, making Lexie's face break out in a smile.

"Mom," she said in a rush of relief.

Her mother opened her eyes and offered the smallest of smiles before closing her eyes again. "Tired," she whispered. Her voice sounded raw but her color was much improved from the last time she had seen her.

"Rest, Mom. I'll be here when you wake up." Lexie brushed her mother's hair from her face and relished in the fact that her mother would be all right. Lexie took a deep breath and stretched her restricted chest and tried to relax her tense physical state. She forced everything else to the back of her mind and concentrated on her mother.

Lexie pulled a chair up beside the bed and watched her sleep. She was trying to keep the weight of everything that was happening at bay. She felt like her sanity was stretched so thin that holes would start developing. She needed to trust in the fact that Jackson was working on finding Stephanie, and that with John currently injured, they did not have to worry about him. She leaned back in her chair and took deep, soothing breaths.

Lexie sat up abruptly when she realized she had fallen asleep, making her head spin. She had no idea what time it was or how long she'd slept. She had been on an adrenaline high for so long she must have crashed. She sat up in the chair and checked on her mother, who seemed to be resting peacefully. Standing up, she stretched her stiff neck and yawned. She desperately needed some caffeine to rouse her drowsy body.

Lexie peeked out into the hallway and down to the waiting chairs visible from where she was. Dane was still sprawled out in an awkward position, trying to sleep on the uncomfortable chairs. She shook her head with a smile before heading his way toward the coffee machine. More people were moving around the halls, indicating a new day had begun. Lexie filled up two cups and then looked in the next machine for something halfway decent for breakfast. She settled on a granola bar and punched in the numbers until the metal arm spun and dropped it to the bottom.

Walking back toward Dane's large body crammed into the small chairs, she tapped his foot with hers. His eyes snapped open and looked up at her before they immediately softened. "Everything good?" he asked, sitting up and looking a little pained.

"Yeah, I got you a coffee and breakfast." Lexie handed him a coffee and the granola bar. "I didn't want to go far, so the options were limited." Lexie tilted her head back toward the vending machines.

"Thanks." Dane's face lit up like she had given

him the greatest present ever. "This is good."

Lexie thought it was strange that he seemed so delighted to receive a disgusting cup of coffee and a stale granola bar. It was like no one had ever given him anything before.

"I'm going back to check on Mom," Lexie said as she turned to head back to the room.

"I'll be here. Just holler," Dane said, ripping open the granola bar and practically eating it whole.

Lexie dropped back into the seat beside her mother's bed with a sigh and took a swig of the coffee. She couldn't help but cringe as the bitter flavour hit her tongue.

"Does it taste that bad?"

Lexie looked up at her mother awake beside her. "Mom." Lexie smiled and reached for her hand. "It tastes so bad but I can't stop drinking it. I think this is my eighth cup since we got here."

Her mother smiled peacefully. "You should try these drugs they gave me, much better than caffeine."

"I bet." Lexie laughed but it quickly died away. "I was worried about you."

"Worrying is my job," her mother responded.

"Not this time," Lexie said, rubbing her mother's hand. "The nurse told me that the surgery went as good as to be expected and you are on your way to a full recovery."

"See, it's not that easy to get rid of me," her mother offered lightly. Even though her mother looked exhausted, she could see her bright light shine through. The sight brought her immeasurable relief.

"There has been something I have been meaning to ask you. Actually there are lots," Lexie confessed.

"I assumed you would have many questions." Her mother wrapped her fingers around Lexie's hand and pulled her closer. "Lay down with me."

Lexie hesitantly crawled up on the side of the bed and gently laid down on her side next to her mother as to not to disturb her injuries.

"This is better," her mother sighed. "Now ask your questions."

"If your last name is really Connors, where did Wilder come from?"

Her mother was quiet for a moment in a thoughtful way. "How much of my diary did you read?"

"Almost all of it," Lexie admitted guiltily.

"Then you know who Dylan was?" her mother asked.

"Yes."

"It was his last name. Dylan Wilder, the man that my heart still loves with every beat," her mother confessed sadly. Lexie wiped a tear away from her mother's face. "He would have loved you, Lexie. He would have been the father you needed."

"You were all I ever needed, Mom."

They remained in a comfortable silence as they held each other. There were so many things to talk about but Lexie just wanted to enjoy this moment. The memory of her wondering if this would be possible again still lingered in her thoughts. She had come too close to losing her mother.

"What's this?" her mother asked, pulling on the

corner of the envelope sticking out of her pocket.

Lexie pulled it out and held it up for them to see. The edges were worn and the paper wrinkled from carrying it around with her. "John gave it to me. It is the results of the paternity test he made me take…" Lexie trailed off as her mother remained quiet. "I can't bring myself to open it."

"Then don't, Lexie," her mother said. "It doesn't change anything."

The door opened and Jackson walked into the room. The sight of him was like a punch to the senses. It was as if she was suddenly dosed in a potent cocktail of fear, anger, and excitement, and the effect left her reeling in confusion. Lexie tucked the envelope back into her pocket and slowly crawled off the bed.

"How are you feeling, Mary?" Jackson asked.

"Please call me Beth. I left Mary in the past a long time ago. I am tired and sore but alive," she offered politely.

Jackson nodded respectfully. "Hopefully I'm not intruding, but I wanted to tell Lexie I got her a room at the motel across the street so she could get some sleep."

Lexie shook her head at the same time her mother replied. "That is a wonderful idea."

Lexie looked at her mother. "I'm not leaving you," she said stubbornly.

"You look exhausted, Lexie, and you're still covered in blood. A little rest and a shower will do you good. I'll still be here when you come back," her mother said softly. The dark circles under her mother's eyes seemed to have darkened substantially in the last few minutes, indicating how tired she really was. "I'm just going to sleep anyway."

Lexie looked down at her stomach where her mother's blood still stained the material. She wiped at it with her hand and realized how much she wanted to change so she didn't have the reminder of what could have happened. Lexie took a deep sigh. "I won't be long."

"Promise me to get some sleep in an actual bed before you come back here, Lexie."

Lexie leaned in and kissed her mother on the forehead. "I love you, Mom."

"I love you too, Baby Girl." Her mother smiled brightly.

"When this is all over I'll help you plant a ton of new flowers in the garden just like we used to," Lexie said brightly.

"Sounds wonderful." Her mother smiled. "I will look forward to it."

"One of my guys will be outside this door if you need anything, Beth," Jackson offered.

"Thank you."

Lexie offered her mother one last smile before she slipped out the door. Dane was standing next to a man she didn't recognize. She assumed it was the stranger that she had seen when they had left the hotel but she was too panicked by her mother's condition to remember any details about him.

"Lexie, this is Nate. He's gonna take over so Dane can get some rest," Jackson introduced. "He's an old friend of mine."

"Hi Nate," Lexie offered politely but she still felt

a little numb, and it was hard to act normal under the conditions.

"It's a pleasure." Nate smiled brightly.

Lexie began walking toward the elevator when she felt Jackson's hand on her shoulder guiding her. She felt unfocused from reality in her exhausted state. Everything blurred together and she fought to stay focused.

When the elevator doors closed, Jackson and Dane both looked at her like she was going to break.

"I'm okay," she insisted. "Stop looking at me like you expect me to burst into tears."

"After sleeping in those shitty chairs, I'm about to burst into tears," Dane said, trying to work out the kinks in his neck.

Lexie looked up at Jackson and was surprised to see so much concern behind his dark eyes. She looked away quickly because the swell of emotion that hit her really did threaten to bring tears. She was still angry at him for betraying her and also extremely grateful to him for saving her and her mother. She was overwhelmed with the war between her mind and her heart and didn't know if she could really trust Jackson, even though she knew she had to. The only thing she knew for certain was Jackson had claimed more of her heart than she intended. If she was honest with herself, she understood why he did what he did. If she had been in his shoes she would have probably done the same.

"I bought us some more time. Evan will be fine." Jackson tentatively touched her arm but then pulled away. He seemed unsure of how to act around her. It was the first time she noticed him being unsure about anything and it surprised her.

Lexie nodded her head. "And Steph?"

"Teddy is working on it."

Lexie took a deep shaky breath. "There is still hope. We are gonna find her, right?" Lexie looked up pleadingly at Jackson.

"Yeah, Lexie, we'll find her."

CHAPTER TWENTY-SIX

Jackson

"After you." Jackson swung the door open to the motel room and waited for Lexie to enter. She walked in and looked around the space until her eyes settled on her purse and her black duffle bag that held her clothes, toiletries, and a large quantity of cash she had shoved inside.

Lexie picked up her purse and pulled out her camera. He could see the visible difference in her shoulders as they relaxed as she ran her fingers over the buttons and turned it on. Jackson remembered watching her take pictures that first day at the cottage. Something beautiful happened when she looked at the world through her lens, she could see things no one else could. She became captivated by the beauty around her and he could see nothing but her.

Lexie turned around and looked at him through

her camera and he looked back at her, wondering what she saw when she looked at him. Did she see the dark, broken man that he was? Did she see his regret that he wore like a heavy weight upon his shoulders? Did she see that he was incapable of walking away from her like he should? Did she see that he wanted her so much if physically hurt him?

She took a picture and lowered the camera, watching him with a closed expression. He wanted to know what she was thinking but he couldn't bring himself to ask. He knew it was only a matter of time until she revealed her anger toward him. He could see it brewing behind those emotion filled eyes. It was like a beautiful calm before the storm.

Jackson scratched the back of his neck. "Did John hurt you?" He saw the storm arrive when he looked into her eyes.

"Did *John* hurt me? What about the person who lied to me and planned to hurt my mother and me? Maybe John is the only reason I'm still alive right now."

"Lexie, I would never—"

"Wouldn't you? I have no idea what you are really capable of." Lexie cut off his words. "What changed? Why are you even here?"

"Because of you," Jackson answered honestly. He was reaching inside a part of him that was a complete stranger to him. His emotions were like trying to read a foreign language and he was scrambling to make sense of them.

"Me? *Me*?" Lexie said angrily. She stomped toward him like a raging storm. "Do you actually feel guilty, you heartless bastard?" When she was close enough, she wound up and slapped him across the face. The sting of it burned across his skin and he welcomed it. "Do you want to hurt me more?" Lexie continued to hit him and he let her land every blow as she worked through the anger that burned a hole deep inside her. He knew he deserved her hatred.

When her assault slowed, her anger melted into tears, and her fight dissipated. Jackson reached for her and pulled her close as he wrapped his arms around her. She tried to push him away but he wouldn't let her. "Listen to me, Lexie. I'm sorry I hurt you. It's something that I will regret for as long as I live, but it was before I knew the truth. I'm here with you now because I'm doing everything in my power to make it right. I can't make you believe me, but I will get you your life back. I will make this right for you." Jackson looked into her tear-soaked eyes.

"I don't know what right is anymore." Lexie shook her head in confusion. "I don't think it can ever be right again."

"That won't stop me from trying." Jackson offered a gentle smile as he brushed her tear away from her cheek with a gentle stroke of his thumb.

Lexie nodded her head and wiped her eyes. "I'm going to take a shower," she whispered. She stepped back from Jackson and he let his hands fall away. He watched her pick up her bag off the bed and walk toward the bathroom.

"Should I go?" Jackson asked, unsure of what she needed from him.

Lexie placed her hand on the door frame and

looked back over her shoulder. "Can you stay?"

"Yes," Jackson replied, surprised by her request. She closed the door and he collapsed into the armchair next to the bed and listened to the sound of the shower turn on. He leaned his head back against the chair and closed his eyes. He wanted to take a moment to enjoy the relief that they had dealt with some of the tension between them. It was hard to focus, knowing that she was furious with him. He couldn't deny the fact that he wanted more, but he would take whatever she gave him. The more time that passed, the harder it was to convince himself that he needed to create distance between them, not encourage a relationship of any kind. His actions did not correlate to his ultimate goal, being he was supposed to walk away when this was all over.

Jackson raked his hands down his face in frustration. He was kidding himself if he thought he could still leave her after this was all done. He never wanted to remember what life was like without her again. She was hope that warmed his battered soul, something he never thought he would have.

Jackson sat up when Lexie walked out of the bathroom. She offered an unsure expression. She looked as if she felt as tormented as he felt, pulled in so many directions he was threatened to be pulled apart. He wondered why now in this time in his life that he would be thrown this curve ball that would completely uproot his whole outlook.

Lexie dropped her bag and the envelope he had seen her staring at slid across the floor. She noticed it as well but didn't move to pick it up. She sat down on the edge of the bed and looked at it like she was hoping it would disappear.

"What is it?" Jackson asked, looking up at her pouted lips and solemn expression.

"It's from John," she whispered. Lexie ran her fingers through her damp hair nervously. She was wearing the same sundress she had worn the first day he had seen her at the cottage as she wandered through the trees taking pictures.

"A part of me needs to know what it says, but another part of me can't stand the thought, so I just keep staring at it, unsure of what will happen if I open it." Lexie finally looked away from the rectangle of paper and up at Jackson.

"What will it possibly change?" he asked curiously.

"Everything and nothing, I guess. I'm scared and I need a drink." Lexie rubbed her forehead.

"That's an easy fix." Jackson offered her a smile and walked over to the bar fridge. He opened it up. "What's your poison?"

"Aren't those little bottles insanely expensive?" Lexie asked, looking at the collection of different labels lined up in the door of the fridge.

"When the situation calls for it, does it really matter?" Jackson grabbed two bottles of whiskey and held one out for Lexie. She looked at it curiously before taking it from him. Jackson sat down next to her on the bed and snapped the cover of his and tipped it to his lips before he glanced over at Lexie. She watched him hesitantly as she unscrewed the cover and brought it to her nose.

"It smells disgusting," Lexie complained.

"It tastes worse." Jackson frowned as he tossed his empty bottle into the small garbage bin across the room.

"Then why do you drink it?"

"I love the rush as it heats my blood." Jackson raised his brow.

Lexie became quiet and looked down at the bottle in her hand. "I know that feeling," Lexie whispered. "That's what it was like when I was with you."

Jackson was surprised that she brought up the history between them. He thought it would be a topic to avoid after what had happened.

"Lex…" Jackson started but she held up her hand to stop him and tipped the bottle to her lips, swallowing the amber colored fluid inside. She covered her mouth and struggled to swallow the harsh liquid before proceeding to cough.

When she collected herself, she looked up at him with watering eyes. "That was horrendous," Lexie protested with a gasp. "You made that look so much better than it deserved."

"You are better than I deserve," Jackson admitted, looking into her eyes and holding them as long as he could.

"How does nothing ever scare you?" she asked, a small crease forming between her brows. Jackson got the urge to press his lips against the spot. He wanted to taste every part of her and savour her always.

"What makes you think nothing scares me?" Jackson asked, his gaze dropping to the small frown that had formed on her full lips. They had a soft sheen from running her tongue along them.

"The way you face everything like you know you will win," Lexie said as she reached up and adjusted the small strap on her shoulder. Jackson couldn't help but follow her movements as he took in her soft skin that smelled of soap and the scent that he had begun to crave upon all else.

"I'm scared right now," Jackson whispered.

Lexie tilted her head in disbelief. "No, you're not."

"I am." He frowned as he reached for the bottle still in her hand. He let his fingers linger on hers before he took the bottle and finished if off. He tossed it into the garbage with the other.

"Why?" Lexie tested him.

"You absolutely terrify me," Jackson admitted.

"I don't believe you." Lexie shook her head with a laugh, like she thought he was teasing her.

"Here," Jackson took her hand and placed it against his chest. Her warm hand pressed upon his skin and he knew she could feel his racing heart. Jackson closed his eyes as she spread her fingers that slipped between the buttons of his shirt and grazed his bare flesh.

"I'm scared too." Lexie pulled her hand away. "I'm scared that once we leave this room everything will change."

Jackson immediately missed her touch. She walked over to the fridge and grabbed another bottle. She didn't even look at the label before twisting off the top and tipping it up to her lips and squeezing her eyes shut. When the bottle was empty, she gasped and covered her mouth. "So gross," she complained, and tried tossing it into the garbage but it missed and hit the wall. Jackson only shook his head and laughed when she grabbed another and did the same.

"Slow down or you will make yourself sick," Jackson offered.

"I don't want to. I don't want to think about anything. I just want you to make me feel how you used to."

Lexie grabbed the hem of her dress and slowly pulled it up over her curves and over her head. Jackson's whole body tensed to the point of breaking as he looked at her standing in front of him with nothing but lacy blue underwear. His body temperature spiked to the point that his clothes felt suffocating.

Her fair skin curved and dipped like a piece of art. Her full round breasts were peaked with pale, puckered nipples that made his mouth water, knowing how sweet she tasted. Scared didn't even begin to describe how she made him feel.

Jackson pushed off the bed but didn't move any closer as he searched her eyes for answers.

"I'm tired of being scared of everything, Jackson," Lexie admitted as she reached for his hand and lifted it against her chest. She pressed his fingers into the soft flesh of her breasts. He could feel the fast thrumming of her heart.

"Please don't be scared of me," Jackson whispered, searching her deep blue eyes.

"How can I not be? I don't even know who you really are."

"I'm trying to fix that." Jackson stepped forward,

searching her expression. He thought this part of her would never be his again. He wanted to show her what it meant to him that she allowed him close. He ran his fingers along her neck and she shivered in response. Jackson leaned down and claimed her mouth with a gentle kiss, slowly savoring her taste as he tried to memorize every detail. He ran his fingers through her hair and pulled her in closer, deepening it. She seemed tentative at first, but any hesitations quickly slipped away as her hands soon grabbed hold of his shirt and frantically searched for the buttons. Jackson pulled back enough to tear his shirt open. The buttons gave way as Lexie pulled the sleeves off his arms and ran her hands over every inch of his chest. A low growl of pleasure erupted from deep within him as he swam in the bliss of her desire.

Jackson placed his hands on her waist and lifted her body against him. She wrapped her legs around his waist and ran her fingers through his hair, devouring his mouth. The feel of her soft skin on his made his groin clench with pooling desire. If there was a heaven, this was it, this was where he wanted to spend his eternity...with the arms of this woman wrapped around him and her need for him desperate in her touch.

Jackson laid her on the bed and looked down at her flushed skin. He placed a kiss on her lips and trailed down her neck. Lexie closed her eyes and Jackson noticed a tear run down the side of her face.

"Hey?" Jackson whispered. "What's wrong?"

Lexie wiped her tear away and looked up at Jackson. "Tell me something real," she whispered.

Jackson lay down beside her and propped himself on his elbow. He grazed the side of her cheek thoughtfully with the back of his fingers and then proceeded to run his fingers over her skin, watching the goosebumps form under his fingertips.

"You are the first person I think of when I wake up in the morning," Jackson admitted as he drew lazy patterns on her stomach. "And the last person I think about before I fall asleep." Jackson looked up into Lexie's eyes. She was quietly staring at him.

Lexie raised her hand and placed it on the side of his face and rubbed her thumb over his bottom lip. Jackson leaned into her touch, desperate for it.

"Will you make me feel good?" Lexie asked.

"I will do whatever you want me to." Jackson leaned down and placed his mouth over her nipple and sucked the taut flesh into his mouth and gently pulled with his teeth until a moan of pleasure escaped her. He ran his hand down her stomach.

Jackson pushed off the bed and slid the material of her underwear down her legs and tossed them aside. Leaning over her, he kissed her belly button and ran his lips over her flat stomach.

"That tickles." Lexie giggled and squirmed under his lips.

Jackson looked up and gave her a sly smile before he moved lower, savouring her soft flesh as he tasted every inch of her. Her hips began to rock under him as he moved closer to her warm center that glistened with her need as he teased and fondled her skin.

When he finally closed his lips around her swollen sex, she moaned and jerked from the pleasure. Jackson's erection throbbed against his pants, raring to feel her, to sink deep inside her, and pull pleasures that could rob a man of everything.

He sunk his fingers deep inside her as he sucked and licked her engorged flesh. He could feel her walls tightening on his fingers as he thrust them deep as she writhed on the bed. Jackson could not think of anything more beautiful than her right now. Her legs clamped around him and her fingers wound tight in his hair as she screamed out in release. A rush of her pleasure ran over his hand as her sweet sex spilled its release on him. He knew he would be forever marked to be hers deep in his soul.

Jackson sat up on his knees and unbuttoned his jeans, pushing them down his thighs. His erection sprung free and hung heavy and swollen with need for her. Jackson kicked his pants off and wrapped his arms around her sated body and pulled her close. He wanted to feel her against him.

She was quiet and he worried what was going through her mind as he held her close. he was terrified she would push him away, so he didn't move. "Tell me something real?" he whispered against her cheek.

"I want you to be gentle," she said quietly against his chest before placing a sweet kiss on his skin.

There were no words that sounded more wonderful. Jackson placed his hands on either side of her face and kissed her soft and deep, telling her what he couldn't find the words for.

Shifting his weight, he guided himself to her warm entrance and slowly pushed inside her body, where his paradise existed. Lexie wrapped her legs around his waist, allowing him to push further until he completely filled her. Jackson kissed her lips as he pressed his thumb against her sex, drawing her pleasure as he pushed and pulled at her core.

Lexie arched her back off the mattress and he closed his mouth over her straining nipples. He could feel her shake beneath him as she succumbed to the sensations. Her unbound desire as she writhed beneath him was the most beautiful sight he had ever seen. He held onto it as long as he could until she screamed out again and he had nothing left to stop the wave of euphoria that hit him.

He was physically spent as if he had run a marathon as he collapsed on his side, rolling Lexie on top of him so he didn't have to break the contact. Once she settled in against his side she sighed in content. He had so many words fumbling around his head wanting to be heard but the call of sleep was too great and he felt himself drift away. He embraced the feeling of happiness that warmed his stomach. This was new for him and he never wanted to let it go.

CHAPTER TWENTY-SEVEN

Lexie

The sound of someone closing a door in the distance pulled Lexie from sleep. For a moment she couldn't remember where she was. Sleep had pulled her under so far that she had no idea where she surfaced. She tried forcing her tired eyes awake but they immediately closed and her body complained. She wanted, more than anything, to pull the covers over her head and shut out the world again.

Then reality reminded her why sleep should be the furthest thing from her mind. Lexie opened her eyes and looked at the empty space beside her. A folded piece of paper sat atop the pillow. Lexie picked it up to read the note.

Come to room 209 when you wake, Sleeping Beauty.

She rubbed her hands down her face and kicked the covers off. The cool air rushed across her skin, reminding her she was naked, and with it thoughts of Jackson heated her skin. She didn't have words for what happened between them. Despite the chaos in the world around them they had found a moment of bliss but now she needed to focus on the world that was still crumbling beneath her feet. Despite her growing feelings for him, Jackson was still very much a wild card in her life. She still needed to be cautious.

Glancing at the clock, she noticed it was 5:46 p.m. She had slept the entire day away. She was anxious to get back to the hospital and also wanted to know if any progress had been made in finding Stephanie. Lexie was determined not to let her imagination wander. She would remain positive and hopeful because anything else would threaten to break her.

Lexie slipped from the bed and noticed her purse on the floor. She picked it up and one of the bottles of deep blue nail polish fell out and rolled across the floor. Lexie stared at them for a moment before tears pooled in her eyes. "Alex," she whispered sadly.

With everything happening she hadn't thought of him until now and the guilt of it began to carve away at her initial flash of relief that she had forgotten about the gaping hole in her heart. She picked up a bottle and sat down on the bed. She unscrewed the cap, letting that familiar scent fill her nose before she lifted her foot to rest on the edge of the bed. She held the brush over her toes with the intention of painting them, but something stopped her. The feel of Jackson against her skin still lingered in her thoughts and it felt realer than anything else. She didn't want to go back to the version of herself that was scared to look in the mirror because she felt guilty she survived and Alex didn't.

Lexie took a deep breath and replaced the cover on the polish. She ran her finger over the label, "Knockout," before setting it on the nightstand. The envelope from John sat propped up against the lamp. Jackson must have set it there. Refusing to touch it, she wiped her tears away with the back of her hand and grabbed for her clothes to get dressed.

Lexie knocked on the room door and took a deep, nervous breath. She didn't have much time to prepare herself before the door swung open and Jackson's dark eyes swallowed her whole. "Hey." He smiled as he stepped outside and closed the door behind him. He placed his hands on either side of her face and pressed his lips against hers. He tasted like mint and whatever insanely addictive smell that always lingered on his skin.

"Hey," she mumbled between kisses. The fire that burned in her stomach was new and intoxicating.

"We have good news," Jackson said, pulling back and grabbing for the handle to lead them inside.

"Do you know where Stephanie is?" Lexie asked in a rush.

"We think so," Teddy answered as he twisted around in his seat to see her enter the room.

Dane was sprawled out on the bed with a pizza box beside him. He gave her a wave as he devoured his slice of pizza.

"Are you hungry?" Dane asked after he swallowed.

"Maybe later," Lexie declined politely. "What did you find out?" Lexie turned back toward Teddy and Jackson, anxious to know what they have uncovered.

"You know how John mentioned that Stephanie will meet the same fate as the girl with the rose tattoo?" Jackson asked and Lexie nodded in return. "In your mother's diary, she mentions a lake house. We managed to track down a property that Masten purchased about thirty years ago. He made an attempt to cover his tracks with transferring it to a bogus name a few years later. He took steps to make sure the property could not be traced back to him but there is always a trail and Teddy found it." Jackson pointed to the aerial view that Teddy had pulled up on the screen. "We think this is the lake house your mother was referring to."

"You read my mother's diary?" Lexie asked, surprised. It wasn't until then that she realized she had forgotten that she had shoved it in her purse before John had taken her. She quickly filed through all the words that still lingered in her mind that her mother had written.

"Yeah, I needed to find the truth," Jackson admitted guiltily.

Lexie wasn't sure what to think of it but the only thing that mattered to her right now was the fact they might have a lead on Stephanie's location.

"I get it," Lexie managed, trying to be understanding. She knew she would have to in his situation. Jackson's reservations seemed to fall away when she offered him a small smile.

"This shot was taken a week ago." Teddy pointed to the screen showing a car parked in the driveway, barely visible through the canopy of trees. "There is definitely activity there."

"We're heading there now," Jackson informed her.

"I want to come too," Lexie added.

Jackson shook his head. "That's not a good idea. You should stay with your mother. She needs you right now.

"But what if she's there and she needs me?" Lexie tried to keep her voice calm but the desperation to find Stephanie betrayed her.

Jackson placed his hand on her shoulder and pulled her closer. "Listen, Lex, it might not be anything at this point. We're going to check it out and see what we find. I promised you I'd find her. You need to let me do this."

Lexie looked into his eyes and nodded. Jackson pulled her close and rested his chin on top of her head. "We'll drop you off at the hospital. We're heading out now."

"Okay." Lexie took comfort in his hold. She believed every word he said. She needed to if she was going to see Stephanie again.

***

Lexie passed by the gift shop in the main entrance of the hospital. Beautiful flowers were displayed in the front window as well as balloons and countless other items that were intended to put a smile on patients' faces. Lexie decided to stop and buy her mother some flowers. She knew her mother would appreciate it.

There was never a time when her mother didn't have fresh cut flowers in her house, whether she picked them up at the local flower shop or cut them from her garden. Her mother loved flowers because she said they reminded her of everything good in life. Lexie decided on a colorful arrangement of flowers that looked like they came from her mother's garden, a complete eclectic assortment. They were bright and cheerful and were sure to put a smile on her face.

Lexie anxiously pushed the button of the elevator and watched the doors close. Her thoughts were with Jackson and the hope that they were right about the location. Lexie was so lost in thought that she didn't even realize she was staring out at her mother's floor. She stepped off just as the doors began to close. This part of the hospital was always so eerily quiet with all the patients recovering from surgery.

When Lexie rounded the corner she was caught off guard when someone ran into her. "Hey," Lexie complained as a man continued to barrel past and caused her to stumble backwards. Lexie caught herself before she fell and looked up to see the man heading quickly toward the stairwell. "What the…" Lexie trailed off, not wanting to yell in the quiet hospital. "A real gentleman," she said sarcastically as she looked down at the floor where broken pieces of flowers were scattered around her feet. Lexie dropped to her knees and tried to pick up the mangled pieces of flowers and tossed them into the nearest garbage can. She looked at her bouquet that showed signs of distress but she managed to straighten them up enough.

Beeping sounds started ringing from down the hall and soon the sound of monitors filled the silence. Lexie glanced down the hall toward her mother's room and her eyes widened in panic as she looked back at the door the man had disappeared behind. "Mom?" Lexie gasped. She started running down the hall when she noticed a nurse hurrying into the room. The flowers slipped from her fingers as she ran as fast as she could toward her mother.

Lexie slid to a stop as she approached the room. The nurse was doing compressions on her mother's chest as she hollered for the other nurses who were rushing past Lexie. Every monitor attached to her mother was screaming and drowning out all the other sounds as Lexie watched in horror.

Her feet felt frozen in place as she watched them try and resuscitate her mother. She looked so small and lifeless on the bed as people swarmed her. She couldn't even understand a word they were saying, it was if they were all talking underwater.

Lexie felt someone touch here arm and Nate's face came into view. His shirt was torn and his lip bloodied. "Lexie?" His face full of concern.

"There was a man…" Lexie whispered. "When I got off the elevator," she continued numbly.

"Where?" Nate grabbed both her arms and spun her around. "Where did you see a man?"

"He ran into me," Lexie pointed down the hall.

"He did something. I know it," she choked on a sob that bubbled in her throat. "He ran toward the stairs."

"Stay here," Nate let go of her and started running in the direction she pointed and disappeared from view. Lexie was left watching the scene unfold before her. Every muscle in her body coiled so tightly she thought she would snap. She didn't understand why her mother wasn't waking up as they worked on her, but the monitors continued screaming. Her mother's doctor came rushing in next but it didn't matter. Nothing any of them did mattered as that continuous flat line rang in Lexie's ears.

***

Lexie didn't remember how she ended up in a room staring up at the white tiled ceiling. Her head felt like it was stuffed with cotton and her memories all felt like dreams as she lazily pushed through them, searching for what was real. She pushed herself into a sitting position and it made her head spin. The lights were off but the illumination from the hall filtered in the room to show she was in a hospital room. She felt like she had just woken from a bad dream as she tried to recollect the details.

The sound of footsteps called her attention. She heard Jackson's voice as he stood just out of view. "Did you see him?"

"No, Lexie did. There was another man that walked in Beth's room before it all happened. When I confronted him, he took off running. When I caught up to him and cornered him, he finally revealed that someone paid him to distract me," Nate's voice trailed off. "I'm so sorry, Jackson. By the time I got back here, whoever was here was already gone. I looked everywhere."

"Fuck," Jackson breathed out in frustration. "How is she?"

"The doctor gave her something that knocked her out because she completely lost it."

Jackson appeared in the doorway and the look on his face said it all. It made all those bubbles burst and she remembered why she was here. "Lexie," her name was a sad whisper on his lips. "You're awake."

Her eyes stung as he became blurry. Lexie dropped her head in her hands just as she felt his arms wrap around her. "I'm here," he said as he scooped her up and held her close. "I'm here."

"Why?" she whispered against his shirt. "Why?"

Jackson pulled her tighter. "I'm so sorry."

CHAPTER TWENTY-EIGHT

Jackson

"Don't leave her side." Jackson looked Teddy in the eyes as he made it very clear how important it was to keep her safe.

"I won't, Jackson. I won't." Teddy reassured him. "I'll take care of her."

Jackson set a glass of water on the nightstand beside the bed before he took one last look at her. Lexie was curled up in the middle of the bed in the hotel room. She hadn't moved since he had brought her here. The doctor had given her pills to take when the other drugs she was administered at the hospital began to wear off. He pulled them out of his pocket and tossed them toward Teddy.

Lexie was in for a rough road and Jackson needed to do everything in his power to find Stephanie now. He knew that's what Lexie would want him to do and he would not let her down.

"Call me when you get anything off those surveillance tapes," Jackson said, grabbing his keys.

"Sure thing," Teddy said, dropping down in the desk chair to continue filtering through the tapes they managed to get their hands on from the hospital. Since they were taken unofficially, Teddy had a lot of footage to sift through until he could find what they were looking for. Jackson wanted to know who was in the hospital.

Jackson followed Dane and Nate and closed the door behind them.

The address of the lake house was a solid forty minute drive from the hotel but Jackson's mind was so full the time didn't seem long enough. It was completely dark outside by the time they approached their destination, providing the perfect backdrop for what they intended to do.

"What are you going to do about Black?" Nate asked, leaning up from the backseat. "We only have a week to get Evan out of there and then there's the other issue?"

"I'll deal with it, Nate," Jackson dismissed it. "Right now we have other concerns."

"What's the other issue?" Dane turned to Jackson.

"The issue should be focusing on finding Stephanie," Jackson tried to dismiss the conversation.

"Jacks," Dane said impatiently.

Jackson looked over at Dane, who already had a suspicious look on his face.

"Black wants Jackson to work for him in exchange for not already killing Evan," Nate answered before Jackson could say a word.

"Jesus Christ, Nate, let me talk," Jackson criticized, shaking his head.

"And if you don't?" Dane asked Jackson.

"Then he'll kill me."

"And not to mention the rest of us," Nate added. "Slash will probably skin us alive."

"Fuck, Nate, enough already." Jackson threw Nate a dirty look over his shoulder.

Nate raised his hands in surrender. "It's the truth. You know Black is gonna make it fucking hurt for all of us."

Jackson rubbed his hand over his unshaven face and sighed. "Black isn't gonna do anything to anyone." He picked up his phone to see the house was only a few minutes out as they pulled onto a dirt road.

"I know you aren't planning on working for Black, Jackson. So what's your plan?" Dane asked after a minute of silence.

"I'm gonna kill him," Jackson answered truthfully.

"At least you're consistent." Dane tilted his head.

They all grew quiet as the road narrowed into a single lane. Jackson continued up the narrow path that drew in tightly around the car. Branches scratched and clawed at the windows as they passed. Fresh tire tracks on the road indicated that someone was either here or had been only just recently. When the drive widened, it opened onto the property in question. A large lake house sat serenely on the calm, evening water. The landscape was in need of care as the grass was overgrown and filled with weeds. The house was framed with a large porch that wrapped around the entire exterior and large windows covered the waterside of the structure. It looked more like a ghost than the beautiful property it should have been.

There were no vehicles on the property and the interior was completely dark when Jackson pulled up to the house and killed the engine. "This place is creepy," Dane said as he looked up at the old grey house.

"You could say that," Jackson agreed. "Let's go." Jackson opened his door and retrieved his gun. Dane and Nate did a quick assessment of the exterior of the property. Everything looked to be in order on the outside and looked over-run by nature. Nothing looked recently disturbed. Jackson ascended the front steps and walked across decking that protested every step. Dane and Nate were at his back, keeping a look out for anything suspicious. Jackson turned the knob on the front door to confirm it was locked before he pulled his gun from his pocket. He hit the glass of the door panel with the butt and reached in to unlatch the door.

Once inside, Jackson pulled a flashlight from his pocket and shone it around the interior. The house was furnished and looked recently used, though the décor was very dated and looked to be original with the house.

"I'll look around upstairs," Dane whispered as he headed toward the staircase off the living room. Jackson nodded and continued down the hallway off the kitchen. Everything seemed to be in order as he checked the rooms until he came to a door at the end of the hall that had a padlock on it. Jackson pulled on it to make sure it was secured before he looked at Nate.

"I'll go find something to open that," Nate said before he headed back outside.

"Check the trunk," Jackson called after him.

A few minutes later Dane walked down the hallway shaking his head. "There was nothing upstairs."

"We might have something," Jackson rattled the lock. "Nate went to get something to open this up."

Nate returned with an axe slung over his shoulder. "I found this next to the wood shed. It'll do the trick, I think."

Jackson and Dane backed away to give him the necessary room as he swung the axe and hit the mark. "You enjoyed that way too much," Jackson commented as he pulled the destroyed lock from what was left of the mangled latch.

Once the door was opened, Jackson raised his gun and started down the narrow steps. It was quiet and the air grew damp as they descended. A door at the bottom of the steps was latched but left unlocked as he turned the handle and pushed it open.

A dim light was set aglow in the far corner of the room but it was enough to reveal what they were walking into. A bed sat against the wall what appeared to be restraints hanging off the headboard, the smell of death was everywhere. Jackson's eyes were drawn to the cell constructed of iron bars in the far end of the room.

A small figure lay on the cot pushed up against

the wall. Jackson lowered his gun and entered the room with Dane and Nate close behind him.

"Jesus," Dane whispered under his breath.

Jackson walked toward the cell as he tucked his gun in his pants. "Stephanie?" he called quietly. He watched her lift her head slightly. After a moment she sat up, holding the blanket against her shivering body.

"Jackson? Is that you?" Her voice was rough and raw. It barely soundly like the same girl he remembered.

"Yes," Jackson grabbed the bars that made up the door and gave them a shake as he looked at the lock. "We need to get this open. Do you know where the key is?"

Stephanie shook her head. "Where is he? He was coming back…"

"Who? Masten?" Jackson asked.

"I don't know his name. He said he would be right back," she whimpered.

"We're here now, Stephanie. He won't hurt you anymore," Jackson assured her.

Jackson stopped moving when he heard a noise upstairs. He turned around and looked at Dane and Nate, who also heard the noise.

"Stay here, Nate," Jackson said as he pulled out his gun and headed toward the stairs. Dane was one step behind him as he made his way up the stairs as quietly as he could manage.

"Who's there?" a man yelled.

When Jackson got to the top of the steps, he nudged the door open that had swung closed behind them. He barely had a chance to glance out into the hallway when a shot rang off, hitting the door from the direction of the kitchen.

"Fuck," Jackson said, ducking behind the door frame.

"Come out!" the man yelled from down the hall. "Come the fuck out of there now, you little shit!"

"I'm unarmed," Jackson called out. "Please don't shoot me."

Jackson listened to his footsteps as he approached. Dane pressed against the wall behind him as his steps drew near the door. Jackson watched the barrel of his gun come into view as the man tried to nudge the door open with his foot.

Jackson grabbed for the gun and managed to get his hand around the barrel and wrench it from his hold as he shoved the door open. Jackson quickly gained the upper hand, swinging his weight around he positioned himself behind Masten and pulled the shotgun up against his neck. Masten struggled to breathe as Jackson held him immobile. Jackson's height gave him the advantage and Masten couldn't gain his footing as Jackson shoved him down the hall and then pushed him down on the floor.

"Please don't hurt me. I'm an important man. What do you want? I'll give you anything."

Jackson brought the butt end of the gun down on his temple and Masten was knocked unconscious from the force.

Dane came around behind him and aimed his gun at Masten's head. "So this sick fuck is the Mayor of Belhaven, huh?"

"Sure is," Jackson spat, searching Masten's body until he recovered a key that might work on the cell he was keeping Stephanie in. "If he moves, shoot him in the legs."

"Be happy to." Dane smirked.

Jackson's phone vibrated in his pocket. He pulled it out to see Teddy's name light up the screen.

"Yeah," Jackson said, placing the phone against his shoulder.

"Find the place?" Teddy asked curiously.

"Yeah, here now, and we're just making the Mayor more comfortable."

"Please tell me Stephanie's there?" Teddy asked.

"Yeah," Jackson confirmed.

"Good, I think Lexie needs the good news."

"Tell her we're bringing her home. What about the tapes?"

"He knew where the cameras were, Jacks. I don't have a clear shot, but if I had to bet money on it, I'd say it's Rosh."

"*Fuck*. I'll call back soon once we get things settled here," Jackson said, ending the conversation.

Jackson met Nate on the stairs as he headed back down. Nate had his gun in hand and seemed overly jumpy. "Watch where you're aiming that thing," Jackson complained as he brushed past him. "You were supposed to stay with her."

"I know, but I thought you might need my help," Nate added. He seemed very unsettled as he followed Jackson back downstairs hesitantly.

Jackson was relieved when the key slid into the lock. Stephanie stood on the other side of the door, anxious to be free of the bars. Even in the dim light he could tell that she had lost substantial weight.

When the door swung open with a loud creak, Stephanie threw herself into his arms. "Get me out of here," she pleaded. "I need to get out." She started to become frantic. Jackson wrapped his arm around her and held her close to his side. Her body shook violently as she clung to him.

"This has been here for a long time. Some real bad shit has happened in this place, I can feel it." Nate visibly got the chills as he looked around.

Jackson picked up Stephanie and cradled her to his chest. "Yeah, I know what you mean. Let's go," Jackson replied tightly. They both wanted to get Stephanie out of here as quickly as possible. Jackson had been in a lot of bad situations and places in his life but this one topped them all. This place was tainted by an evil that snaked its way into your bones and gave you chills. Jackson could hear the whispers of malicious acts that had been committed behind these walls. It was something he would never be able to shake.

Jackson carried Stephanie through the main room where Dane was still holding Masten at gun point. "He's coming to," Dane warned him.

"Rose..." Masten mumbled. "Where are you taking her?" Masten tried to sit up but Dane kicked him back to the ground. "Don't take my Rose."

Nate stalked over to Masten and aimed his gun at his head. He looked possessed by hatred that Jackson didn't know Nate was capable of.

"What are you doing, Nate?" Jackson asked with warning.

"I'm gonna kill this sick motherfucker," Nate seethed, his gun shaking in his hand. He stared down at Masten cowering on the floor. His appearance was far from the man who had such a high regard in the city of Belhaven as he squirmed on the floor and reeked of alcohol. This was the other side of him that hid in the shadows that they only just shone a light on. Unfortunately, Jackson had a feeling that while they managed to save Stephanie, it was not soon enough for others.

"Back off, Nate. We're not killing him," Jackson demanded.

Dane stepped closer to Nate. "This fucker is going to pay for what he did, slowly and painfully, I promise." Dane placed his hand on Nate's arm. "Put the gun down."

Stephanie buried her face in Jackson's chest, terrified to see the man who had abducted her, and began to sob. Nate looked back at her and then finally submitted. He lowered his gun and stepped back. "You promise he'll suffer?" Nate clenched his jaw as his wild eyes looked at Jackson.

"I promise."

"What do we do now, Jacks?" Dane asked as he looked down his gun at Masten. The man began blubbering for his life, begging them to spare him as he offered money and promises. They all ignored his pleas. Dane kicked him back down when he tried to grab for Dane's leg.

"Tie him up. We're gonna call this one in," Jackson said as he stared down at Masten. "This fucker deserves to be exposed and we are not gonna let him off easy like his brother."

"*You?*...it was you who killed Seth?" Masten narrowed his eyes. He tried to push of the ground but Dane knocked him back down.

"You won't be so lucky, Masten," Jackson responded as he turned to leave, knowing Stephanie needed to get out of this house and away from the man who terrorized her.

CHAPTER TWENTY-NINE

Nate

Masten cursed as Nate pulled the ropes tight. A satisfied smile curled the edges of Nate's lips as he reveled in the enjoyment of causing Masten pain as he secured him without mercy to a chair he grabbed from the dining table. The man was practically frothing at the mouth as he continued to plead for them to let him go. "I will do anything," Masten begged over and over again with promises of money and power.

"Shut the fuck up," Nate said as the pulled the last of the ties tight. Dane stood with his gun aimed at Masten's head, not taking any chances until he was completely secure. Nate rounded the chair to get a look at his handy work. It would be impossible for Masten to get out of these ties.

"Those are some serious boy scout knots," Dane said with an appreciative frown.

"Like I went to boy scouts." Nate shook his head with a snort. Masten's eyes widened as Nate wound up and swung his fist, connecting with the mayor's nose. Nate could feel the snap of cartilage as pain rang up the length of his bones in satisfaction. "And done," he said, shaking his fist.

"What was that for?" Dane asked with a raised brow.

"Just testing to see if everything was secure." Nate wiped his hand on his pants. "I'm gonna go check on Jackson and the girl," he said as he headed toward the door, anxious to get out of the house. Something about being in this house made him extremely unsettled. If sadness could take form it would be the shadow that swallowed this house.

As soon as Nate pushed through the front door he could feel the weight lift from his shoulders and the temperature change was astonishing. He hadn't realized he was so cold until he walked out into the humid air and his body welcomed the heat. His bones practically hurt from the chill.

Stephanie was curled up in a blanket sitting in the backseat of the car as she stared at a bottle of water that her hands were wrapped around. She looked so small and broken and it pained him to see her in that condition. None of them knew what Masten had done to her but his imagination did not do him any favors. He had to keep his mind from wandering because he wouldn't be able to stop himself from marching back in that house and emptying his gun into that man. When he had called Stephanie "Rose," it set him off. Hearing that name was like a knife to the heart. His nerves had been frayed before but he had been so close to pulling the trigger.

Another car was parked partially onto the lawn with its driver's side door open. The headlights cast strange shadows over the overgrown lawn. Nate looked down at his feet when he kicked something. He looked down to see a grocery bag with food items scattered across the porch.

Jackson was on the phone with a man named Giles when he approached. When he saw Nate he nodded and walked away from the car so Stephanie could be spared further details that he needed to pass along. Nate walked up to her and leaned down next to her. "You don't know me, but my name is Nate. I'm a friend of Jackson's," he offered quietly. "Let me know if I can do anything to make you more comfortable until paramedics get here."

She looked up at him and her sad eyes completely floored him. He wasn't sure if she could speak even if she wanted to. She looked too haunted and exhausted from the trauma she endured. Nate noticed something on her neck.

"Are you hurt?" He pointed toward a mark on her neck as it peeked out from under the blanket.

She shook her head slightly and grabbed the blanket with a shaky hand to reveal a tattoo on her neck. "He…did it," she whispered through a raw throat. "I don't know." A tear fell down her face.

Nate stared at the tattoo and couldn't breathe when it felt like he was hit in the chest. He knew what it was. He knew exactly what that was because he had looked at it every day for as long as he could remember. Nate dropped back on his hands and then scrambled to his feet as he ran toward the treeline. He barely made it before he emptied the contents of his stomach violently. His body kept insisting on heaving long after there was nothing left. He placed his shaky hands on his knees for support as he listened to the sound of sirens approach, growing louder and louder as he squeezed his eyes shut and tried to stop the flood of thoughts that assaulted him and made him want to throw up again despite the fact he had nothing left.

"Nate," Jackson called to him. "You okay, man?"

Nate managed to nod his head and wipe his mouth with the back of his hand. The world felt off balance as he made his way back to the car. He felt almost drunk as he watched two police cars pull into the driveway, followed only a minute later by an ambulance. He stood watching as Jackson addressed and then directed the paramedics toward Stephanie.

The paramedics dropped their bags by the car and began to assess the traumatized girl still huddled in the backseat. Nate stood numbly by the side as more emergency vehicles piled onto the property, as they parked in every available area and the headlights soon lit up the entire place. Shadows danced around on the house and Nate could only stare at it as he shook with a chill that drilled deep inside him.

Jackson glanced over at him as he led the officers inside the property but he still couldn't move. "Do you need medical assistance?" A female paramedic appeared in front of him.

He looked down at her and shook his head. "No," he offered numbly.

He watched her back away hesitantly as if unconvinced until finally she turned her attention back toward the others treating Stephanie as they helped lay her on a stretcher.

Nate reached into his back pocket and pulled out his wallet. Opening it, he pulled out a photograph he had folded and tucked inside. The only picture he had of his mother before she had disappeared when he was a small boy. He ran his thumb over her likeliness and the rose tattoo she had on her neck. The exact same tattoo that Stephanie had. All the hope that he had carried all these years completely vanished.

CHAPTER THIRTY

Twenty-Three Years Ago

Rose

The cramps have been getting worse. Rose knew this day would come and she prayed she would have more time. Her baby could not come into the world like this. Not into this cold, dark dungeon that had become her life. As time had passed and her stomach continued to grow, she never let go of the hope that she would be found. She refused to believe that this was all she would ever know again. She needed to know her baby would be safe and have a life outside these walls.

Her captor, Terence, never talked about the baby. It was as if he pretended she wasn't carrying a child. She was terrified what would happen when the baby was born and now she had run out of time.

She had tried so hard to please him, make him believe she cared for him. She knew that's what he wanted from her. He wanted her to love him and so she would swallow the terror that filled her chest and endure the pain for fear of what would happen if she did not. She endured countless horrors that haunted her dreams and reminded her of the hell she was cast into. The life inside of her and what she left behind were the only things that kept her strong. Her children were the only thing that made her open her eyes every day and never let the hope fade.

As long as she kept him happy, the pain was more bearable and the life inside her was not threatened. She forced a smile on her face and pretended she was happy to appease her captor but it was all for her child. She did not want it to be created in a body filled with constant fear. She needed to fool herself into thinking that she was content and this man would not break her.

Rose curled up on the bed with her hand pressed against her hardened stomach as she breathed through the pain. "Please, please, please..." she chanted over and over again. "Not now," she sobbed into the pillow. She lost track of time as she drowned in the constant pain of contractions as they hit her over and over without mercy. Her prayers were left unheard as the baby made its way into the cold hell that had become her life.

Rose didn't even hear him enter, didn't know he was standing just outside the bars watching her until she heard his voice between her gasps and whimpers of pain.

"Rose?" Terence called to her.

Rose cringed and shuffled back on the bed until the cold wall pressed against her. The sound of the door creaking open stole her breath and the pain intensified through her stomach and wrapped around her back as if she were being torn in two.

She could feel his hands on her but she was too delirious from the pain to care. "What's wrong, Rose?"

"The baby," she gasped between strangled breaths.

Terence lifted her up and carried her out to the bed that housed her nightmares. The feel of it caused fear to wash over her and she screamed out as a contraction hit her hard and fast.

"I can help you," he said, brushing the sweat-soaked hair from her face. He left her side and started shuffling around in the drawers in the cabinets in the far side of the room. Rose rolled on her side and tried to breathe through the pain. He turned on another lamp and lit the dim room enough to see.

Rose's gaze immediately found the unlocked door. He had forgotten to lock the door and for the first time she felt a flicker of excitement deep inside her stomach that pushed the pain aside and took center stage.

She turned toward him to see him approach with a tray of cloths and various things that he set next to the bed. Her eyes landed on the scissors that were resting on the edge of the tray. She looked at him, and for the first time since he had locked her away, she noticed he was the one who looked scared. He sat down next to her on the bed and pulled her nightdress up to reveal her bare stomach. He placed his hands on her and the feel of his touch made her sick. Like a disease trying to infect her. She knew he thought this baby was his but it wasn't. She had just discovered she was pregnant the day she had been taken. She hadn't even had a chance to tell anyone but her son. She prayed her husband and son didn't think she abandoned them.

She knew she couldn't stay bound in these walls forever, slave to a man who slowly carved away at her sanity for his own sick needs. She needed to find a way to break free and save her unborn baby before it was too late. She desperately wanted to go home.

Rose grabbed for the scissors and lunged at him without another thought. She could feel the blade sink into the tissue of his neck but she had missed and the blade punctured shallow as it tore through the skin. The shock in his cold, dark eyes cause her to act quickly. She didn't have time.

She scrambled off the bed, grabbing for her stomach that was clenching violently. The pain made her eyes water. She ran as fast as she could manage as she pushed through past the agony. She could hear him stumble after her calling her name, but she didn't slow. She swung the door open and climbed the stairs. She used the railing to pull herself faster. The adrenaline coursing through her body was battling the ache that carved deep into her pelvis and back. Her legs did not want to cooperate but she forced them to keep moving as her feet slapped heavily on the floor. She ran through the house, unsure of which direction to turn but the sight of the front door brought tears to her eyes as she ran toward it.

She opened the door and ran out into the fresh air

that felt amazing on her stale lungs. She gulped it greedily as she hurried over the porch boards and down onto the soft grass. Spinning on her feet, she looked toward the trees.

Terence came barreling through the front door as he grasped his neck. Rose grabbed her stomach and ran as fast as she could. She wove through the trees and tripped on the uneven ground. Branches pulled and scratched at her as she ran through the forest cast aglow by only the moon above her that filtered through the tall branches. The pain radiated down her legs and she could feel the pressure start to burn between her legs. Rose tried to push her hand against herself as she struggled to keep moving but she knew she would have to stop. She could feel the warm fluid rush through her fingers as she stumbled and she grabbed a tree for support.

Sliding down to the ground, she reached between her legs to feel the head of her baby. Tears of joy and horror poured from her eyes. The pressure was overwhelming as she bore down. She tried to not make a sound as she pushed through the pain.

Rose reached down and grabbed hold of her baby as the shoulders released and pulled it up into her arms. She had known he was a boy from the moment she first felt him inside her. Tears washed down her cheeks as she kissed his wet face. His cries, although beautiful, would bring her captor to them. She cradled her baby, holding him tight as she felt her body grow tired. She moved her feet on the ground and noticed how much blood she was losing. Something was terribly wrong and she couldn't deny it.

Fear spiked her heart and made her head feel like it was underwater. "No…" she gasped as she saw Terence's figure emerge through the trees. She could feel herself dying and she had no way to protect her baby from the evil that was coming.

To be continued…

ACKNOWLEDGEMENTS

A huge thank you to:

My family, who are always my biggest fans.

Limitless Publishing, for giving me the opportunity to share this series with the world.

Toni Rakestraw, my fabulous editor, who has to fix all of my annoying writing habits.

Author J.L. Drake, for being wonderful.

Dawn Canfield, Hot Pressed Books, for her great advice.

My reader group, Aimee's Amazing Aces, who are endlessly lovely and supportive!

Readers, these were only words upon the pages until you brought them to life.

ABOUT THE AUTHOR

Aimee McNeil was born and raised in Nova Scotia, Canada, where she continues to live today with her husband and three children. She is a stay-at-home mother that loves every colorful moment with her family.

Aimee spends most of her free time indulging in her love of writing. You can also find her lost in the pages of a good book, or making a mess with her paints. Aimee loves to explore anything that promotes creativity. It is one of the many reason she enjoys writing.

Facebook:
https://www.facebook.com/aimeemcneilswriting

Twitter:
https://twitter.com/aimeeswriting

Website:
http://www.aimeemcneil.com/